Introduction

It's a genuine delight to make this unusual collection of proverbs available. There are 3,650 of them and if you read ten a day you'd read them all in a year, but that's not the point. These proverbs also provide a wealth of raw material for composing Triku (see the next section) but that's not the point either. *3,650 of the World's Finest Proverbs* represents a carefully chosen, balanced survey of the proverbial wisdom of the world, and that's the point! This collection of humanity's insights from around the world and through the centuries offers amusement, wisdom and guidance to everyone who consults it.

These "World's" greatest proverbs are actually from Africa, Asia and Europe. There is no intent to slight the Americas and "Oceania," they may be represented in a subsequent volume. However, this work is limited to those three continents. In fact, Africa, Asia and Europe provide the structural arrangement of the book.

This continental framework has some interesting implications. For instance, Turkey is as much a part of Asia as China is, though they are rarely thought of as representing the same area. In many ways northern Africa has more in common culturally with the near East (in Asia) than with sub-Saharan Africa. Still, Morocco and Egypt are in Africa, not Asia. Biblical proverbs are classified as Asian, but Yiddish proverbs are European! The fact is—any scheme of arrangement is going to be ragged around the edges. Fully recognizing this, we've stuck with the simple, continental distinction, hoping that these groupings and contrasts will shed light on fundamental similarities and subtle differences of the human experience.

The thematic arrangement was another challenge. Working with elements, such as "Day & Night" and "Song & Dance" we have arranged these proverbs to encourage subtler contrasts and interplays. Since "Earth & Sky" is not your ordinary proverbial category, some proverbs are set side-by-side which would normally never be thought of together. The resulting juxtapositions add additional flavor to the banquet of wisdom.

The themes we've chosen are not parts of a grand system. Like proverbs themselves, we cover the basics of human experience—"Fathers & Mothers," and "Laughter & Tears." However, moving out from that center, the themes become more serendipitous. As we sorted the proverbs, we took subjects as they came; for example, "Long & Short" presented itself, but "Early & Late" did not.

At the conclusion of each "chapter" there is a selection of ten proverbs under the heading of either "Odds & Ends" or "He who & She who." These catch-all categories salt the arrangement with randomness and humor. Here we have taken an editorial liberty by re-phrasing some gender neutral proverbs which began "He who..." to begin with "She who...". This was done in a spirit of balance since, in the world of proverbs, as in so many other arenas, the female experience has been severely underrepresented.

We welcome your comments and questions. Just email:

3650proverbs@triku.com

We have worked hard to accurately record authentic proverbs (see the bibliography for a list of sources). The careful reader will notice some variation in the way a proverb's origin is identified. Sometimes it's by country (India), sometimes it's by language (Hindi). Sometimes it's just by continent (African) and there are a few identified by religion (Islamic). Since we wanted this work to be dependable as well as enjoyable, we were never more specific than our sources.

The most common proverbs of Western culture have been excluded. *The New Dictionary of Cultural Literacy* (Third edition, 2002) lists two hundred and fifty-six proverbs in general use (e.g. A penny saved is a penny earned.; Two heads are better than one.). Not one of them is among the 3,650 in this collection. We have also worked to exclude duplicate proverbs—even cross-cultural duplicates. Of course this has involved some judgement calls, but we think we've succeeded. Please let us know if you think you've spotted one...er two. If we agree (there are some *judgment* calls), we'll correct it and thank you by name in the revised edition.

The pursuit of these goals has resulted in a collection of proverbs unique in breadth, depth and presentation. Whether for personal edification, a timely quote, or just for fun, we believe *3,650 of the World's Finest Proverbs* will be a source of insight, encouragement and delight for everyone who uses it.

Enjoy the feast!

Christopher J. Stuart
Triku.com LLC

3,650
of the
World's Finest
Proverbs

Order additional copies on the web at
www.triku.com
or
BookSurge,LLC
www.booksurge.com
1-866-308-6235
orders@booksurge.com

Book design by Richard G.Wagner

3,650
of the
World's Finest
Proverbs

Compiled by
Christopher J. Stuart

2 0 0 5

Contents

Introducing **Triku**™

Triku is a newly defined format for saying things. You can learn all about it by visiting Triku.com. Here's a brief explanation of Triku and it's relation to *3,650 of the World's Finest Proverbs*.

Triku is a format for saying things which is defined by three rules:

1) A triku has three phrases;

2) Each phrase of a triku is seven syllables;

3) The phrases of a triku must form a plausible sentence in any of their six possible arrangements.

Here is an example:

If the king says it is night / In the middle of the day / Look up and behold the stars

Christopher J. Stuart

This is a triku in its primary form. Since the three phrases can occur in any one of six possible arrangements, the other five forms of this triku are:

If the king says it is night / Look up and behold the stars / In the middle of the day

In the middle of the day / Look up and behold the stars / If the king says it is night

In the middle of the day / If the king says it is night / Look up and behold the stars

Look up and behold the stars / If the king says it is night / In the middle of the day

Look up and behold the stars / In the middle of the day / If the king says it is night

Though a triku should be able to stand on its own as a reason-ably insightful statement, by rearranging the phrases, a variety of things happen. As a mental exercise, the words and meanings reassemble into something similar but different. Statements may become questions and questions become statements. In some triku the terms assume different grammatical functions depending on the order of the phrases. There's a meditative aspect as the central meaning of the triku is poured through the different arrangements, like moving a diamond around to catch the light at different angles.

The name "Triku" is an adaptation of "Haiku." Haiku is a traditional form of Japanese poetry which consists of three lines totaling seventeen syllables in a 5/7/5 pattern. Triku is not an attempt to improve or update Haiku. "Triku" simply recognizes and seeks to honor its common ground with Haiku. Both forms are composed of three lines with strict meter: Triku has 21 beats in a 7/7/7 pattern. Beyond this they diverge. Haiku is a traditional form of poetry whose goal is to evoke the feeling of the experience the words describe. Triku is a new form of expression which can communicate almost anything.

Triku.com emphasizes the presentation of proverbs, epigrams and witty sayings as triku. But the form is not limited to this. One could compose a triku as a love poem, a recipe, an advertising slogan or a memorial. Triku is a format for sayings: in the broadest sense of the term, "something that is said."

A distinguishing aspect of Triku is that the author of every triku is identified and the copyright on every triku is registered. In other words, if you compose a triku and post it at Triku.com, your composition will be registered with the U.S. copyright office and you will be officially and forever recognized as the author!

The connection between Triku and *3,650 of the World's Finest Proverbs* is simply that these proverbs provide a rich source of raw material for composing triku. For example "If the king says it is night / In the middle of the day / Look up and behold the stars" is developed from the Arabian proverb "If the king says that it is night in the middle of the day, look up at the stars" (Odds & Ends, page 96). Composing a triku based on a proverb and then claiming original authorship may seem like plagiarism. It most certainly is not. The effort required to form the thoughts within the three line, seven syllable, interchangeable constraints of Triku ensures originality. Admittedly, it doesn't look like it required much work to form that triku, but after you've tried it yourself, you'll appreciate the creative effort and mental energy involved.

Here are some other examples. "All men have three ears, one on the left of his head, one on the right and one in his heart." is an Armenian proverb (found in "Eyes & Ears" page 47). That wisdom, recast as a triku is:

Each one of us has three ears

Two on the sides of our head

One that's deep within our heart

Christopher J. Stuart

You can mentally rearrange the phrases yourself (or visit Triku. com and watch the phrases rearrange themselves). As you do, you'll find the meaning comes through with a slightly different emphasis which may shed additional light on the insight at the heart of the triku.

A river loses its name

When it runs into the sea

No matter how great it was

©Triku.com   Christopher J. Stuart

This triku was inspired by the Ghanian proverb "Every river that runs into the sea loses its name" (Earth & Sky, page 37). You can see how the essential point is built upon by including the contrast of the river's greatness. The Mississippi is no less absorbed than the humblest of streams. And all this is crafted into the three-line, seven-beat interchange-ability of a triku.

The Wolof proverb "Even the fall of a dancer is a somersault" (Song & Dance, page 161) illustrates how the idea of a proverb can be maintained while being significantly rephrased in a triku.

If you do it gracefully

You can manage to look good

Even as you trip and fall

©Triku.com   Christopher J. Stuart

Visit Triku.com to see more triku and to find out how to explore and enjoy this new art form.

Whether or not you have any interest in Triku, *3,650 of the World's Greatest Proverbs* will be a source of insight and enjoyment. But, if you're interested in composing triku, these proverbs provide a mother lode of raw material which you can refine into your very own, officially registered, expressions of wisdom.

A beautiful thing is never perfect. -Egyptian

As soon as you obtain the thing, it loses its beauty. -Ghanian

Because of the beauty of a new thing,
the parrot put scarlet on its chest. -Ghanian

Man is not handsome when he becomes old. -Ghanian

The surface of the water is beautiful,
but it is no good to sleep on. -Ghanian

"You are ugly." is different from "You are very ugly." -Ghanian

The good looking man is king, if there is no rich man near. -Hausa

If you are ugly be winsome. -Tunisian

An old rice bag is ugly, but the thing inside is beautiful. -Kpelle

The ornaments of the doctor have no beauty. -Lugbara

Ugliness has called you by name, you answer, "Yes." -Lugbara

Every country has its beauty. -Moroccan

There is no beauty but the beauty of action. -Moroccan

If there is character, ugliness becomes beauty;
if there is none, beauty becomes ugliness. -Nigerian

If you find "Miss This Year" beautiful, then you'll find
"Miss Next Year" even more so. -Nigerian

The beauty of moonlight
doesn't enable you to pick up a needle. -Nkundu-Mongo

In a land where hunchback people abound,
he who goes straight up is ugly. -Oromo

The ugliness of the person on horseback is seen only
by those on the ground. -Oromo

Though looking nice, the heifer does not give good milk. -Oromo

The beauty of the corn cob is apparent in the inside only. -Swahili

Like a gold ring in a pig's snout is a beautiful woman
who shows no discretion. -Biblical

If you want to take revenge on a man,
send him a really beautiful woman. -Arabian

A woman gets thirty percent of her beauty from nature
and seventy percent from makeup. -Chinese

Beautiful roads never go far. -Chinese

Beauty does not ensnare men; they ensnare themselves. -Chinese

Even ugly faces are worth looking at—
and that is a great comfort for most people. -Chinese

If the pedestal is beautiful
the statue must be even more beautiful. -Chinese

A beautiful bride
needs no dowry. -Iraqi

The homely woman is precious in the home, but at a feast
the beautiful one is preferred. -Chinese

Ugly wives and stupid servant girls
are treasures above price. -Chinese

No bride is ugly on her wedding day. -Hebrew

A beautiful woman belongs to everyone;
an ugly one is yours alone. ~Indian

Apple blossoms are beautiful, but rice dumplings are better. ~Japanese

Even beautiful things have disadvantages
and must be used with caution. ~Japanese

In the eyes of a lover a pockmarked face
is one with pretty dimples. -Japanese

What is good is not necessarily beautiful. -Japanese

Only a certain amount of flowers and jewels are beautiful. -Tibetan

A heart in love with beauty never grows old. -Turkish

He whom the heart loves is the handsome one. -Turkish

A plain woman with moral beauty
is better than a beautiful woman. -Vietnamese

A beautiful face is admired
even when its owner doesn't say anything. -Danish

Beauty is but a blossom. -English

It is a blind man's question to ask
why those things are loved which are beautiful. -English

One cannot make soup out of beauty. -Estonian

The ugliest tomcat always has the most beautiful mate. -French

There are no beautiful prisons or ugly loved ones -.French

Who loves ugliness will not encounter beauty. -German

Beauty and Chastity are always quarreling. -Spanish

That which is loved is always beautiful. -Norwegian

Time has no respect for beauty. -Polish

Beauty without wisdom is like a flower in the mud. -Romanian

Every family has its own ugly member. -Russian

Desire beautifies what is ugly. -Spanish

Her father's fortune will make the ugliest girl attractive. -Spanish

She who loves an ugly man thinks him handsome. -Spanish

There is no pot so ugly but finds its cover. -Spanish

Youth has a beautiful face and old age a beautiful soul. -Swedish

A homely girl hates the mirror. -Yiddish

Better to have an ugly patch than a beautiful hole. -Yiddish

The ugliest life is better than the nicest death. -Yiddish

3

A blind man doesn't care if lamp oil is expensive. -Armenian

A dog in a kennel barks at his fleas—a hunting dog does not feel them. -Chinese

A chicken that hatches a crocodile's eggs is looking for trouble. -Madagascan

A centipede though dead will not fall. -Japanese

A cat may go to a monastery, but will always remain a cat. -Ethiopian

A bed free from anxiety is the most agreeable of all things. -Tamil

A boat doesn't go forward if each one is rowing his own way. -Swahili

A cat likes to eat fresh fish but it will not go into the water. -Mongolian

A canoe does not know who is king. When it turns over, everyone gets wet. -Madagascan

A cemetery never refuses a dead man. -Lebanese

After every affliction there is enjoyment. -Moroccan

A grave is not dug before a person dies. -Zulu

Don't provoke your in-laws before sleeping with your wife-to-be. -Bemba

Choose the neighbor before the house,
and the companion before the road. -Moroccan

Do not dispose of the monkey's tail before he is dead. -Congolese

Don't take a second mouthful
before you have swallowed the first. -Madagascan

Do not measure up the wood before the tree is cut down. -Madagascan

Before firing, you must take aim. -Nigerian

After looking
at its rear-end,
the **elephant**
eats a tree. -Oromo

How lovely is the sun after rain, and how lovely is laughter
after sorrow. -Tunisian

A person dies before we appreciate him. -Jabo

After vomiting there is no nausea. -Ghanian

When you arrive in a village they love you,
but after three days watch how they treat you! -Ghanian

It is before the wind comes that the elephant grass is motionless. -Ghanian

The ceiling is swept before the floor. -Ghanian

After an injury to the heart, an animal is killed
and shared to make peace. -Oromo

After the hyena passes the dog barks. -Oromo

After the war has passed, "I will buy a spear," says the fool. -Oromo

The rain stops in May, after that prayers cannot bring it. -Oromo

The tail and regret come after. -Oromo

Man's affairs are evaluated only after his coffin is closed. -Korean

Reckon the climb before reckoning the descent. -Lebanese

Before you beat the dog, find out the name of his master. -Chinese

Dig a well before you are thirsty. -Chinese

Before you prepare to improve the world, look around
your own house three times. -Chinese

Do not eat before you have fed your animal. -Hebrew

It is little use to dig a well after the house has caught fire. -Indian

After eating nine hundred rats, the cat is now going on a pilgrimage. -Indian

After victory,
tighten your
helmet chord. -Japanese

Before you let your voice be heard, first lick your lips. -Indonesian

Have patience, everything is difficult before it gets easy. -Iranian

After three years even a disaster can be good for something. -Japanese

More festive than the feast itself is the day before. -Japanese

Tap even a stone bridge before crossing. -Korean

Carve the peg only after studying the hole. -Korean

Measure your throat before you swallow a bone. -Chinese

Cast your bread upon the waters,
for after many days you will find it again. -Biblical

A man's body buried in the snow will after a time come to light. -Chinese

A good name comes after a while,
but a bad name is soon obtained. -Kashmiri

The first drink of cold water after intoxication is unknown to the teatotaler.
-Japanese

Don't sell the bearskin before the bear is dead. -Dutch

Choose your company before you drink. -English

One day before you is better than ten years behind you. -Russian

After a time even a dog makes a compromise with the cat. -Hungarian

After great droughts come great rains. -Dutch

Think on the end before you begin. -English

Coming events cast their shadows before. -English

It is afterwards events are understood. -Irish

One may go a long way after one is tired. -French

After a trial, one party is naked and the other without a shirt. -Serbo-Croatian

After a good cry, your heart is lighter. -Yiddish

Light your lamp before night overtakes you. -Greek

One look before is better than two behind. -Irish

The droplet is always at its largest just before it drops. -Bulgarian

After pleasant scratching comes unpleasant smarting. -Danish

Wait until it is night
before saying that it has been a fine day. -French

After high floods come low ebbs. -Dutch

Regretting the past is like chasing after the wind. -Russian

One hour's sleep before midnight is worth two after. -English

A rotting tree leans long before it falls. -Finnish

He whose mother is naked is not
likely to clothe his aunt. -African

She who always eats the roots
of a plant is capable of any
thing. -Chinese

He who would make a fool of
himself will find many to help
him. -Danish

She who always goes after birds
does not ask about their nests.
-Ghanian

He who would have his will let
him cultivate patience. -Welsh

She who answers is inferior to
the one who asks the question.
-Indian

She who always thinks it is too
soon is sure to come too late.
-German

He who works as a slave,
eats as a king. -Indian

She who argues builds no roads.
-Ovambo

He who would be rich should
not collect money, but reduce
his needs. -Spanish

Even a small axe is better than striking with a stick. -Ovambo

However old the horse, it is better than new sandals. -Hausa

Ignorance that supports me is better than
wisdom which I must support. -Egyptian

A little subtleness is better than a lot of force. -Congolese

Being happy is better than being king. -Nigerois

To spend the night in anger is better than to spend it repenting. -Wolof

Spilled water is better than a broken jar. -Wolof

Avoiding a quarrel is better than asking forgiveness. -Hausa

A slip of the tongue is worse than a slip of the foot. -Ghanian

Work for the sake of the children is better than
pilgrimage and the holy war. -Moroccan

I have eaten tiger nuts, I have eaten sugar cane.
Sugar cane is better than tiger nuts. -Ghanian

A libel hurts worse than a spear thrust. -Hausa

The soup would be none the worse for more meat. -Sudanese

If something happens to you, don't be uneasy about it,
for perhaps what is coming will be worse. -Ghanian

To be disappointed is worse than not going at all. -Ghanian

When a man gets rusty, he is worse than iron. -Ghanian

There is no worse curse than to desire a man's death. -Efik

Not to know is bad, not to wish to know is worse. -Wolof

It is worse to be wounded by words than a sword. -Moroccan

A self-made fool is worse than a natural one. -Gikuyu

One calamity is better than a thousand counsels. -Turkish

One evening's conversation with a superior man is better than
ten years of study. -Chinese

A jungle inhabited by fierce tigers is better than
a country ruled by a cruel tyrant. -Tamil

A single ripe pear is better than a whole basketful of unripe pears. -Kashmiri

One lamp in a dark place is better than
lighting a seven-story pagoda. -Chinese

To quarrel with a man of good speech is better than
to converse with a man who does not speak well. -Sanskrit

The end of a matter is better than its beginning. -Biblical

A bad daughter-in-law is worse than a thousand devils. -Japanese

They are worse off at the end than they were at the beginning. -Biblical

A stone thrown at the right time is better
than gold given at the wrong time. -Iranian

Good wood is better than a good layer of painting. -Vietnamese

Half a fool is worse than a whole one. -Hebrew

The more you add, the worse it gets. -Hebrew

The bigger a man's head, the worse his headache. -Iranian

It is worse to excuse than to offend. -Indian

Love from someone who is bad is worse than his hatred. -Indian

Too much is worse than too little. -Japanese

No one sews a patch of unshrunk cloth on an old garment, for the patch
will pull away from the garment, making the tear worse. -Biblical

10   A shepherd that is free from debt is better than a penniless prince. -Turkish

It is impossible to be worse off than a teacher. -Chinese

If it doesn't get better, depend on it, it will get worse. -Yiddish

The king's chaff is better than other people's corn. -English

Experience without learning is better than
learning without experience. -English

A small fish is better than a large cockroach. -Russian

The higher the house, the worse the storm. -Norwegian

An imaginary illness is worse than a real one. -Yiddish

The better lawyer, the worse Christian. -Dutch

Learning makes a good man better and an ill man worse. -English

A good retreat is better than a poor defense. -Irish

The more shepherds there are, the worse the flocks are watched. -German

Working on the land is better than praying in the desert. -German

The old age of an eagle is better than the youth of the sparrow. -Greek

Bad is called good when worse happens. -Norwegian

One time "here you are" is better than ten times "heaven help you." -German

An iron peace is better than a golden war. -Polish

Men are just as God made them—and a little worse. -Spanish

A titmouse in the hands is better than a crane in the sky. -Russian

A trout in the pot is better than a salmon in the sea. -Irish

The worse the carpenter, the more the chips. -Dutch

The more you stir, the worse it will stink. -English

A faultfinder complains even that
the bride is too pretty. -Yiddish

A man believes that he has been born,
he does not believe that he will die.
-Turkish

A lazy man does not know he is
lazy till he drives a tortoise away
and it escapes. -Hausa

A hungry dog will bring a lion down. -Turkish

A little work is better
than a large quarrel. -Oromo

A good memory is not so good
as a little ink. -Chinese

A judge who is on your side
is worth more than a hundred
witnesses. -Iranian

A letter is half a visit. -Iranian

A kitchen knife cannot carve
its own handle. -Korean

A man does not live a hundred
years, yet he worries enough for
a thousand. -Chinese

A big bird cannot be trapped with chaff. -Shona

The bird is not big until he spreads his wings. -Jabo

A great matter puts a smaller out of sight. -Yoruba

If a small mole appears, catch him,
even if you are hunting for its mother. -Swahili

If it's a big man that is hurting you, smile at him. -African

The portion that a man keeps for himself is usually not the smallest. -Congolese

Never marry a woman who has bigger feet than you. -Bantu

A big fish is caught with big bait. -Sierra Leonean

The **more help** in the cornfield
the smaller the harvest. -Zimbabwean

You arrive Mr. Big Shot but leave Mr. Nobody. -Zulu

Small termites collapse the roof. -Ovambo

Give thanks for a little and you'll find a lot. -Hausa

It is a small thing that is taken to measure a big thing. -Ashanti

Many small rivers make the ocean big. -Ghanian

If the eyes of the praying mantis are bigger than its body,
it becomes ugly in appearance. -Ghanian

If small streams come together, it is called a river. -Ghanian

A small fire burnt the entire house. -Lugbara

The small path brings a person to the large path. -Oromo

A small axe will fell a big tree. -Nkundu-Mongo

Do not despise a gift no matter how small it is. -Basotho

Serious disasters come from small causes. -Japanese

A great fortune depends on luck, a small one on diligence. -Chinese

A little for you and a little for me—this is friendship. -Kashmiri

The frog at the bottom of a well believes
that the sky is as small as a lid of a cooking pot. -Vietnamese

Whoever knew you when you were small will not respect you
when you're big. -Arabian

No matter how big, one beam cannot support a house. -Chinese

You can't load a small boat with heavy cargo. -Chinese

Draw the bow but don't shoot—
it is a bigger threat to be intimidated than to be hit. -Chinese

A great forest is set on fire
by a small spark. -Biblical

Great things can be reduced to small things, and small things
can be reduced to nothing. -Chinese

No matter how big the sea may be, sometimes two ships meet. -Chinese

A man who cannot tolerate small ills
can never accomplish great things. -Chinese

Water does not stick to the mountain,
and vengeance does not stick to a big heart. -Chinese

People seek out big shots as flies seek out the elephant's tail. -Indonesian

A man finds what he takes to be small;
it will only be big again when he loses it. -Indonesian

The big drum only sounds well from a distance. -Iranian

A fish gets bigger when it gets away. -Japanese

The smallest pepper is hottest. -Malaysian

However big the whale may be, the tiny harpoon can rob him of life. -Malaysian

If you take big paces you leave big spaces. -Burmese

It would be a very big book that contained
all the maybes uttered in a day. -French

Only in dreams are the carrots as big as bears. -Yiddish

Big fish are caught in deep waters. -Serbo-Croatian

At a little fountain one drinks at one's ease. -French

A little gall embitters much honey. -Spanish

Mend the hole while it is small. -Serbo-Croatian

Two small lobsters make a big one. -Manx

Even a small star shines in the darkness. -Finnish

A little body does often harbor a great soul. -English

The udder of a neighbors' cow is always bigger. -Serbo-Croatian

Small people always cast big shadows. -French

No bed is big enough to hold three. -German

Howling makes the wolf bigger than he really is. -German

Where there is no bridge the smallest plank is of great value. -Hungarian

What is the use of a big wide world
when your shoes are too small? -Serbo-Croatian

In small churches, small saints are big. -Slovenian

Who stumbles without falling makes a bigger step. -Spanish

In a small house God has His corner,
in a big house He has to stand in the hall. -Swedish

The best ointment comes in small boxes. -Walloon

Little sticks kindle the fire, great ones put it out. -English

He who will not work of his own accord
will find himself forced to work by another.
-Hausa

He who wants what God wants of
him will lead a free and happy life.
-Japanese

He who wears trousers of
iron will not sit down. -Fulani

He who was born to be hanged will
not be drowned, unless the water go
over the gallows. -Danish

She who asks questions,
cannot avoid the answers.
-Cameroonian

She who betrays you is not
one from far away. -Afican

She who begins ill finishes
worse. -Italian

She who begins a conversation, does
not foresee the end. -Mauritanian

He who who gives you a fish at
high water season is a true friend.
-Nkundu-Mongo

She who at first suffers afterwards finds ease. -Turkish

The senior brother is the one in charge. -Ghanian

Your brother who hates you is like
someone else's brother who loves you. -Ghanian

When one goes to war, it is with one's brothers. -Ghanian

A brother is the eye on the back of your head. -Lugbara

"Although I am thin I am the brother of a broad spear,"
said the needle. -Oromo

Darkness is a brother to a thief. -Basotho

Who throws stones at night, kills his own brother. -Beninese

Fire has no brother. -Nigerian

A brother is like one's shoulder. -Somalian

Brothers love each other when they are equally rich. -African

No one, because of respect, marries someone's sister
who has a deformed waist. -Ghanian

Your mother's child is your real brother or sister. -Ghanian

If your sister is in the group of singing girls,
your name always comes into the song. -Ghanian

If your sister is beautiful, she is not so for you. -Ghanian

The son resembles the mother's brother;
the daughter resembles the father's sister. -Oromo

The wealth of the brother does not save
the sister from gathering cabbage. -Oromo

The bald woman boasts of her sister's hair. -Tunisian

Anger towards a sister is only flesh deep not bone deep. -Igbo

If the thief is not ashamed, his sister will be ashamed. -Igbo

Theft and poison are sisters. -Lugbara

An angry man is a brother of the madman. -Lebanese

Silence is the brother of acceptance. -Lebanese

Live together like brothers and do business like strangers. -Arabian

A dog by your side is better than a brother miles away. -Iranian

Profit is the brother of loss. -Turkish

An offended brother is more unyielding than a fortified city. -Biblical

A man of many companions may come to ruin, but there is a friend who sticks closer than a brother. -Biblical

To beat a tiger one must have a brother's help. -Chinese

Even brothers keep careful accounts. -Chinese

When you are in difficulty, go to the house of your friend— not your sister's. -Indian

Brothers and sisters are like hands and feet. -Vietnamese

A thousand men may live together in harmony, whereas two women are unable to do so although they be sisters. -Tamil

The friendship of a brother-in-law lasts while one's sister lives. -Tamil

Two scorpions living in the same hole will get along better than two sisters in the same house. -Arabian

The girl who gets married is no relative anymore. -Korean

A family without a daughter is like an oven without heat. -Korean

The eldest daughter is a baby sitter for her younger siblings. -Vietnamese

Blessed the house where the daughter arrives before the son. -Hebrew

How good and pleasant it is when brothers live together in unity. -Biblical

Say to wisdom, "You are my sister," and call understanding your kinsman. -Biblical

Two happy days are seldom brothers. -Bulgarian

The younger brother has the more wit. -English

The younger brother is the better gentleman. -English

A good friend is worth more than a bad brother. -Serbo-Croatian

Go not every evening to your brother's house. -Spanish

A landmark is very well placed between the fields of two brothers. -French

Onion and garlic are born brothers. -Russian

Profit and loss are twin brothers. -Estonian

When I had money everyone called me "brother." -Polish

Between brothers, two witnesses and a notary. -Spanish

Beauty is the sister of idleness and the mother of luxury. -Russian

When a needle sees a dagger, she cries "o sister!" -Russian

Well-married is when you have no mother-in-law and no sister-in-law. -Spanish

Beauty's sister is vanity, and its daughter lust. -Russian

The brother would rather see the sister rich than make her so. -English

Despair and hope are sisters. -Slovenian

Good health is the sister of beauty. -Maltese

Custom and law are sisters. -Slovakian

In the house where there are two girls, the cats die of thirst. -Romanian

One daughter helps to marry the other. -Italian

19

A razor may be sharper than an axe, but
it cannot cut wood. -African

A rose too often smelled loses
its fragrance. -Spanish

A nail secures the horseshoes, the shoe the
horse, the horse the man, the man the castle,
and the castle the whole land. -German

A river never flows straight. -Tamil

A man does not run among thorns for
no reason; either he is chasing a snake
or a snake is chasing him. -African

A man travels as far in a
day as a snail in a hundred
years. -French

A mule driver is not aware
of the stink of his animals.
-Yemeni

A pregnant woman wants
toasted snow. -Hebrew

A man who was always complaining was quite
rightly sent to hell. "Why are you burning
damp wood?" was his first comment. -Arabian

A person does not lay on one side
throughout the sleep. -Annang

A gun is not so hard to buy as powder: A gun is bought one day, powder must be bought again and again. -Yoruba

Making money selling manure is better than losing money selling musk. -Egyptian

The wolf doesn't concern himself with the price of a sheep. -Hausa

Through lack of bargaining one loses a cheap buy. -Hausa

A blind man needs not to buy a mirror. -Fulani

Choose your neighbor before you buy your house. -Hausa

If you do not suffer from the compulsion to buy, you also do not suffer from the compulsion to eat sweet things. -Ghanian

God **gives, but he doesn't sell.** -Burundi

No one sells his laying hen without a good reason. -Ashanti

Nobody pays the bridal price of thirty six dollars for a woman and then sleeps alone. -Ghanian

A thousand camels cannot buy a loving blessing. -Oromo

Don't buy a boat that is under water. -Congolese

If power can be bought then sell your mother to get it. You can always buy her back later. -Ghanian

Truth came to market but could not be sold; however, we buy lies with ready cash. -Yoruba

If you buy what you see, one day you will see something you really want to buy and will be put to shame because you have no money. -Ghanian

If the prices are equal, choose the best. -Moroccan

Good things sell themselves; those that are bad have to be advertised. -African

Witch doctors do not sell their potions to each other. -Bantu

If you go to the market and there are two antelope thighs hanging there and you buy one, you don't bargain for the one left. -Ghanian

If you reduce the price of something, you do so to collect ready cash. -Ghanian

Gold buys silver, but silver does not purchase gold. -Hebrew

The grocer does not open his shop for the sake of one customer. -Turkish

A man without a smiling face should not open a shop. -Chinese

Merchants regard each other as foes. -Japanese

If you buy cheap meat, you'll smell
what you have saved when it boils. -Arabian

If there are many buyers in the market,
the merchant doesn't wash his turnips. -Chinese

From Nanking to Beijing, buyers are never as smart as the sellers. -Chinese

If you don't want to be cheated, ask the price at three shops. -Chinese

May both seller and buyer see the benefit. -Turkish

Though the emperor be rich, he cannot buy one extra year. -Chinese

To open a shop is easy—the hard part is keeping it open. -Chinese

When prices drop, buy. -Hebrew

Deceive me about the price but not about the goods. -Indian

Honey is one thing, the price is another. -Turkish

When you go out to buy, don't show your silver. -Chinese

"It's no good, it's no good!" says the buyer;
then off he goes and boasts about his purchase. -Biblical

Money can buy a lot that is not even for sale. -Chinese

If I had two loaves of bread, I would sell one and buy hyacinths,
for they would feed my soul. -Islamic

The buyer repents, the seller also repents. -Turkish

A melon seller never cries "bitter melons"
nor a wine seller "thin wine." -Chinese

The bargainer buys, not the praiser. -Slovenian

Better buy than borrow. -English

He that buys land buys many stones; he that buys flesh buys many bones;
he that buys eggs buys many shells;
but he that buys good ale buys nothing else. -English

It is good to buy when another wants to sell. -Italian

Whether you buy or not, you can always barter a little. -Russian

There are more foolish buyers than foolish sellers. -French

A good crop, sell early; a bad crop, sell late. -Russian

What costs nothing is worth nothing. -Dutch

One eye is sufficient for the merchant, but a hundred
are scarcely enough for the purchaser. -Basque

God sells knowledge for labor, honor for risk. -Dutch

One may buy gold too dear. -English

He that could know what would be dear
need be a merchant but one year. -English

There are more buyers than connoisseurs. -French

A man trying to sell a blind horse always praises its feet. -German

You don't learn anything from buying, but you do from selling. -Russian

Cheap things cost a lot of money. -Spanish

Buy from desperate people, and sell to newlyweds. -Spanish

It is no sin to sell dear, but a sin to give ill measure. -Scottish

He that refuses to buy counsel cheap, shall buy repentance dear. -English

23

Don't sell the skin till you've caught the bear. -Dutch

He who wants to sell his honor will always find a buyer. -Arabian

He who walks with the wise grows wise, but a companion of fools suffers harm. -Biblical

She who cannot carry the stone must roll it. -Swedish

He who wants to bring home the riches of India, he must have them within himself. -Spanish

She who buys useless things, later sells things that he needs. -Japanese

She who can squint looks into the bottle. -Ghanian

She who can handle a writing brush will never have to beg.
-Chinese

She who boasts much can do little. -Nigerois

He who wants a new world must first buy the old. -Dutch

He who wants to be happy must stay at home. -Greek

A borrowed cloak does not keep one warm. -Egyptian

Money knows no day on which it is not welcome. -Shona

Three kinds of people die poor: those who divorce, those who incur debts, and those who move around too much. -Wolof

A promise is a loan. -Ovambo

If you buy something and have to sweat before you pay for it, then you are pleased with yourself. -Ghanian

A borrowed thing will not fulfill your desire. -Fulani

The poor man cannot sell nor buy. -Ghanian

Borrowing is a wedding, paying back is mourning.
-Swahili

Better sell cheap than for credit. -Hausa

If women say you are handsome, it means you are going to incur debts. -Ghanian

If you buy something and pay for it with ready cash, it is as if you bought nothing. -Ghanian

Poverty without debt is real wealth. -African

Money is sweet balm. -Egyptian

If you pay your debts, you get peace of mind. -Ghanian

If you are in debt to your soul and have not paid this debt, your soul gets angry with you. -Ghanian

Money kills more than do weapons. -Nigerian

If a poor man has nothing else, at least he has a tongue with which to defer the payment of his debts. -Ghanian

Part payment should not make the creditor sad. -Ghanian

It is constant refusing to pay a debt that causes the kidnapping of someone from the debtor's town. -Ghanian

If someone says he will give you something sweet to eat and he gives you money, he has done it. -Ghanian

25

A debt is extinguished by force of paying,
a journey by force of walking. -Turkish

With money you are a dragon, without it you are a worm. -Chinese

Borrowed garments do not fit well. -Japanese

Money makes even a bastard legal. -Hebrew

With money you can influence
the spirits; without it you cannot summon a man. -Chinese

Money can build roads in the sea. -Arabian

Good manners can be paid for with compliments, but only the sound of
money will pay your debts. -Chinese

Money hides
a thousand deformities.
-Chinese

Shame is forgotten, debts are not. -Chinese

Don't visit auctions if you have no money. -Hebrew

The money you dream about will not pay your bills. -Indian

There are four things in this life of which we have more than we think:
faults, debts, years and enemies. -Iranian

A borrowed cat catches no mice. -Japanese

Better to wash an old kimono than borrow a new one. -Japanese

Money grows on the tree of persistence. -Japanese

Making money is like digging with a needle. Spending it is like pouring water
into sand. -Japanese

A thousand regrets do not pay one debt. -Turkish

Salt is good to eat anywhere in the world; money is good to use anywhere
in the world. -Chinese

The borrower is servant to the lender. -Biblical

All earthly goods we have only on loan. -Arabia

Beauty is potent, but money is omnipotent. -English

Better to go to bed supperless than to rise in debt. -English

When death comes, the rich man has no money,
the poor man no debt. -Estonian

Everyone must pay his debt to nature. -German

He that dies pays all debts. -English

He is young enough who has health, and he is rich enough
who has no debts. -Danish

It is not so good with money as it is bad without it. -Yiddish

Where money talks, arguments are of no avail.
-German

Money does not smell. -Russian

Money is the best soap—it removes the biggest stain. -Yiddish

If you have no money, be polite. -Danish

Three things come into the house uninvited: debts, age, and death. -German

Does your neighbor bore you? Lend him some money. -Italian

Don't put money in your purse without checking it for holes. -Portuguese

The art of doing business lies more in paying than in buying. -Spanish

Debts are like children, the smaller they are the louder they scream. -Spanish

With money in your pocket, you are wise, handsome
and you sing well too. -Yiddish

For sins, you cry; but for debts, you pay. -Armenian

Speak little, speak truth; spend little, pay cash. -German

A hundred years of regret pay not a farthing of debt. -German

27

A sheet of paper is lighter if two of you don't try to carry it. -Korean

A trick is clever only once.
-Yiddish

A single stick may smoke, but it will not burn. -Ethiopian

A wise man won't call a fool a fool, but a fool will always call a wise man a fool. -Russian

A thousand masters, a thousand methods. -Chinese

A single grain makes the balance heavier. -Egyptian

A skilled artisan is not fussy about the material.
-Japanese

A trap without a bait catches nothing. -Swahili

A single stone is enough for a house of glass
.-Iranian

A sparrow suffers as much when it breaks its leg as does a flanders horse. -Danish

If a ram is brave, its courage comes from its heart, not its horns. -Ghanian

When you have courage, you shoot an elephant. -Ghanian

If one throws what one has in hand, one will not be a coward. -Oromo

One does not have to cross a flooded river to show bravery. -Basotho

The little ant at its hole is full of courage. -Bemba

An army is driven back by courage and not by insults, however many. -Ashanti

Who is brave enough to tell the lion that his breath smells? -Berber

Blood is the sweat of heroes.
-Zimbabwean

A brave man is scared of a lion three times:
first when he sees the tracks; second when he hears the first roar;
and third when they are face to face. -Somalian

At the place of a coward there is nothing to eat. -Basotho

The man who is all alone has no courage. -Ghanian

The saying is: "Fear has long life," not "Courage has long life." -Ghanian

The courageous sheds blood; the coward sweats. -Lugbara

Trickery is not cowardice. -Basotho

One who does what he says is not a coward. -African

Even over cold pudding, the coward says: "It will burn my mouth." -Ethiopian

A coward sweats in water. -Ethiopian

A coward is full of precaution. -Somalian

A coward has no scar. -Zimbabwean

The mother of the coward does not grieve for him. -Egyptian

29

Have no fear of sudden disaster or of the ruin
that overtakes the wicked. -Biblical

In the heart of every brave man a lion sleeps. -Turkish

Men of principle have courage. -Chinese

Bravery without intelligence is not bravery. -Arabian

The righteous are bold as a lion. -Biblical

Fate assists the courageous. -Japanese

A lion knows no danger. - Tamil

To threaten the brave with death is like promising
water to a duck. -Arabian

When danger approaches, sing to it. -Arabian

Courage is a kingdom without a crown. -Hebrew

All the water in the sea doesn't even reach the knees of the man
who fears not death. -Indian

When the cat gets too old, the mice are not afraid any more. -Burmese

As the pine and the cedar endure the frost and snow,
so intelligence and wisdom overcome dangers and hardships. -Chinese

Under a brave general there are no cowardly soldiers. -Japanese

When you have no choice, mobilize the spirit of courage. -Hebrew

The wicked man flees though no one pursues. -Biblical

If you spit in the face of a coward he'll tell you that it's raining. -Lebanese

Fear is the fever of life. -Sanskrit

Demons strike the timid. -Tamil

The wild grass fears the frost, and the frost fears the sun. -Chinese

Let him not be a lover who has not courage. -Italian

A good anvil is not afraid of the hammer. -Greek

A bold attempt is half success. -Danish

Courage vanquishes some sufferings and patience the others. -Finnish

It is courage that vanquishes in war, and not good weapons. -Spanish

Heroism consists in hanging on one minute longer. -Norwegian

The fox will catch you with cunning, and the wolf with courage. -Albanian

Courage cannot be bought at the inn. -Corsican

Fortune favors the bold. -English

One with the courage to laugh is master of the world
almost as much as the one who is ready to die. -Italian

Who has no courage must have legs. -Italian

Despair gives courage to a coward. -English

Many are brave when the enemy flees. -Italian

Make a coward fight and he will kill the devil. -English

Cowardice will not prolong life. -Laplandish

Between two cowards, he has the advantage who first
detects the other. -Italian

A courageous foe is better than a cowardly friend. -English

For compassion and for cowardice there is no remedy. -Yiddish

Better be a coward than foolhardy. -French

The virtue of a coward is suspicion. -English

He who uses bad incense must be
careful not to burn his sleeves.
-Arabian

She who complains much does
little. -Swahili

He who took the donkey
up to the roof should
bring it down. -Lebanese

He who trades with a two dollar gold
weight does not ask for meat that
costs five pesewas. -Ghanian

He who trusts in himself is a fool,
but he who walks in wisdom is kept
safe. -Biblical

She who carries too much
tenderness will become a slave.
-Burmese

She who cannot sleep can
still dream. -Ivorian

She who chatters with you will
chatter about you. -Egyptian

She who cannot suffer discom-
fort, will not be called for important things. -Chinese

He who travels a lot be-
comes wise; he who is wise
stays home. -Chinese

In the morning the mouth smells, but there are good words in it. -Oji

One who marries for love alone will have bad days but good nights. -Egyptian

You must decide where you are going in the evening,
if you intend to leave early in the morning. -Mali

The sun does not miss a day. -Lugbara

No one ever kept looking for a sleeping place until dawn. -Ghanian

You don't see a person in the daytime and then at night light a lamp
to look at his face. -Ghanian

No one knows what a new day will bring forth. -Ghanian

No one says good morning before the rooster. -Ghanian

When the rains fall at night and you do not hear it, don't you see
from the ground the next day? -Ghanian

A lie is like darkness; truth like daylight. -Oromo

At dawn one goes to visit the family one thought about
during the night. -Oromo

The hyena, knowing what it did to the people at night,
flees from them in the daytime. -Oromo

The person who has seen a snake during the day
flees from a strip of leather at night. -Oromo

The praise of God in the morning is not enough for the evening. -Oromo

Though they refused the advice of the old man in the morning,
they returned to it in the evening. -Oromo

One can know the day one goes but cannot know the day one returns. -Oromo

Truth, like the dawn, will be exposed in time. -Oromo

Where one spends the night is more important than
where one spends the day. -Oromo

The one who has something to eat in the morning is the one who
saved some from the evening before. -Nkundu-Mongo

Affairs are healed by the light of day. -Basotho

33

The day has eyes and the night has ears. -Lebanese

Men ought not to be one day without employment. -Chinese

This morning knows not this evening's happenings. -Chinese

To get up early for three mornings is equal to one day of time. -Chinese

You must start by night to arrive by day. -Iranian

Dawn does not come to awaken a man a second time. -Arabian

Choose your inn before dark, get back on the road before dawn. -Chinese

Even the most beautiful morning cannot bring back the evening. -Chinese

Last night I made a thousand plans,
but this morning I went my old way. -Chinese

Night hides a world but reveals a universe. -Iranian

The loss of one night's sleep is followed
by ten day's of inconvenience. -Chinese

Since love departs at dawn, create, O God, a night that has no morn. -Indian

If you carry treasure, don't travel at night. -Japanese

Without women there is no day and no night. -Japanese

Make your whole year's plans in the spring, and your day's plans
early in the morning. -Chinese

The path of the righteous is like the first gleam of dawn, shining ever
brighter till the full light of day. -Biblical

Don't love the moon more than the sun. -Thai

A good breakfast cannot take the place of the evening meal. -Chinese

Do not leave to morning the business of evening. -Turkish

Man's mind changes morning through evening. -Korean

Butter is gold in the morning, silver at noon, and lead at night. -English

Every day has its yoke; every hour its work. -Estonian

Every day is a messenger of God. -Russian

In the evening one may praise the day. -German

The evening crowns the day. -English

Lose an hour in the morning and you'll be all day hunting for it. -English

A foul morning may turn to a fair day. -English

The muses love the morning. -English

What is done by night appears by day. -English

New day—new destiny. -Bulgarian

What is true by lamplight is not always true by sunlight. -French

Brandy is as lead in the morning, silver at noon, and gold at night. -German

Darkness and night are mothers of thought. -Dutch

The world is nonsense: what looks beautiful in the morning
looks ugly in the evening. -Maltese

The night rinses what the day has soaped. -Swiss

Take your thoughts to bed with you, for the morning
is wiser than the evening. -Russian

It is day still while the sun shines. -English

Do not blame the sun for the darkness of the night. -Georgian

Everything may be bought except day and night. -French

35

Merry nights make sorry days. -English

As people go their own way,
destiny goes with them. -Tamil

Be the town ever so far there is
another beyond it. -Fulani

At the house of the hyena don't seek
to borrow meat! -Oromo

All things seem difficult at first. -Chinese

As drinking coffee requires a
snack so talking with a king
requires a gift. -Oromo

Anything that releases you
from a dilemma is useful. -Fulani

All brides are beautiful;
all the dead are pious. -Yiddish

As long as you stay in a group, the
lion will stay hungry. -Nigerian

An inch in an hour is
a foot a day. -English

Anybody with any sense doesn't go to
a funeral and then laugh when he gets
up to leave. -Ghanian

No matter how full the river, it still wants to grow. -Congolese

The river may dry up but she keeps her name. -Nigerian

A forest that has sheltered you, you should not call a patch of scrub. -Oji

The jungle is stronger than the elephant. -Wolof

No dew ever competed with the sun. -Zulu

It rained on the mountaintop, but it was the valley below that got flooded.
-African

The barking of the dogs will not disturb the clouds. -Berber

Every river that runs into the sea loses its name. -Ghanian

Rain beats on a leopard's skin, but it does not wash out the spots. -Ghanian

The stone in the water does not know how hot the hill is,
parched by the sun. -Nigerian

The sun is the king of torches. -Wolof

If one stone is piled on top of another, it is called a mountain. -Ghanian

When the river floods over, the fish become daring. -Ghanian

One does not climb a tree to welcome the rain. -Oromo

Those who live on the mountain worship it; others cut firewood on it. -Oromo

To give birth is to dig a mountain. -Basotho

The rainbow is not God but it prevents God sending rain. -Hausa

One day's rain makes up for many days' drought. -Yoruba

"The person who does not like my clouds, will not like even my rain,"
said the Lord. -Oromo

The best trees grow on the steepest hills. -Burundi

37

The little hill of a low district becomes a mountain. -Turkish

The tiger depends on the forest; the forest depends on the tiger. -Cambodian

Follow the river and you will get to the sea. -Indian

For he who has the time even the jungle is a paradise. -Tamil

Rivers and mountains may easily change, but human nature
is changed with difficulty. -Chinese

Though God is almighty, he doesn't send rain from a clear sky. -Afghan

Where the sun shines, there is also shade. -Indian

As long as the clouds don't weep, the pasture cannot laugh. -Iranian

The drowning man is not troubled by rain. -Iranian

Sun is for cucumbers, rain for rice. -Vietnamese

Rocks need no protection from the rain. -Malaysian

Whoever watches the wind will not plant;
whoever looks at the clouds will not reap. -Biblical

A country may go to ruin but its mountains and streams remain. -Japanese

No forest without a bear. -Turkish

Men trip not on mountains, they stumble over stones. -Hindustani

Though the wind blows, the mountain does not move. -Japanese

Sunshine without rain makes a desert. -Arabian

Any water in the desert will do. -Arabian

However much snow falls, still it does not endure the summer. -Turkish

Clean out the drainpipes while the weather is good. -Chinese

Use your eyes in the field and your ears in the forest. -Latvian

Fame, like a river, is narrowed at its source and broadest afar off. -English

A mountain and a river are good neighbors. -English

Even God cannot make two mountains without a valley in between. -Gaelic

The mountains make the mists and the valleys must consume them. -German

The river's reputation ends where the sea begins. -Russian

In large rivers one finds big fish but one may also be drowned. -Spanish

It's good to watch the rain from a dry standpoint. -Dutch

It is the great north wind that made the **Vikings.** -Norwegian

Do not push the river; it will flow by itself. -Polish

When the sun is highest it casts the least shadow. -Italian

We all see the same sun, but we don't eat the same meal. -Russian

A shadow is a feeble thing but no sun can drive it away. -Swedish

To a crazy ship all winds are contrary. -English

If you're afraid of wolves, don't go into the forest. -Russian

In time of drought even hail is welcome. -Greek

The smallest of clouds can hide the sun. -Armenian

The wind gathers the clouds and
it is also the wind that scatters them. -Romanian

The calendar is made by man; the weather by God. -Swedish

Change of weather is the discourse of fools. -English

39

To know a man well one must
have eaten a bushel of salt
with him. -French

We must suffer much, or
die young. -Danish

What is the use of running
when you're on
the wrong road? -German

Try not to get hold of a
leopard's tail, but if you
do—don't let go. -Ethiopian

Walk fast and you catch
misfortune; walk slowly
and it catches you. -Russian

Two people fit easier into
one grave than
under one roof. -Slovakian

Try this bracelet: if it fits you
wear it; but if it hurts you,
throw it away no matter how
much it sparkles. -Kenyan

To the ant, a few drops
of dew is a flood. -Iranian

Uphill one climbs slowly;
downhill one rolls fast. -Yiddish

40

Water which is not sufficient
for bathing in is not sufficient
for drinking. -Ghanian

It is difficult to beat a drum with a sickle. -Hausa

It is easy to cut to pieces a dead elephant, but no one dares attack a live one. -Yoruba

The neighbor's field is easy to hoe. -Ovambo

The mouth is easy to open but difficult to close. -Shona

Only the man who is not hungry says the coconut has a hard shell. -Ethiopian

Nothing is so difficult that diligence cannot master it. -Madagascan

"Let me see you do it." makes the performance difficult. -Ghanian

However hard a thing is thrown into the air,
it always falls to the ground. -Nigerois

The shrub with one root is not hard to pull up. -Hausa

Difficult tasks call for strong men. -Shona

It is difficult to stay with someone who is not your relative. -Ghanian

It is not difficult to fill a child's hand. -Ghanian

It is easy to share two things. -Ghanian

A good yam is not difficult to cook. -Ghanian

A matter settled beforehand is not difficult to be adjusted. -Ghanian

The tree which is near a stone is difficult to cut down. -Ghanian

It is easy to get troubles, but not easy to find a helper. -Ghanian

Wrongdoing is not difficult. -Ghanian

A good case is not difficult to state. -Ghanian

If you throw two stones into the air, it is difficult to catch them both. -Ghanian

41

An army of a thousand is easy to find,
but, ah, how difficult to find a general. -Chinese

To win the battle is easy; to secure the victory, difficult. -Korean

To bow the body is easy; to bow the will is hard. -Chinese

To die is easy, to live is hard. -Japanese

The door of charity is hard to open and hard to shut. -Chinese

It is easy to go from economy to extravagance; it is hard to go from
extravagance to economy. -Chinese

To know how to do it is simple, the difficulty is in doing it. -Chinese

A good drum does not have to be beaten hard. -Chinese

Beginning is easy
to keep going is hard.
-Japanese

The door to virtue is heavy and hard to open. -Chinese

It is hard for an ex-king to become a night watchman. -Indian

Riddles already solved look easy. -Iranian

If you like to have things easy, you'll have difficulties; if you like problems,
you will succeed. -Laotian

The way of the unfaithful is hard. -Biblical

To establish a business is easy; to maintain it, difficult. -Korean

Even a clever daughter-in-law finds it hard to cook without rice. -Chinese

Forethought is easy, but regret is difficult. -Chinese

A resolute man cares nothing about difficulties. -Tamil

It is easy to dodge a spear in the daylight, but it is difficult to avoid
an arrow in the dark. -Chinese

To pour out water is easy, to gather it up is difficult. -Chinese

What was hard to bear is sweet to remember. -Portuguese

It is easy with a full belly to praise fasting. -Serbo-Croatian

To blame is easy, to do it better is difficult. -German

It is easy to keep a castle that has never been assaulted. -English

It is easy to bid the devil be your guest, but difficult to get rid of him. -Danish

To fall is easy; to get up is difficult. -Swedish

It is hard to drive a hare out of a bush in which he is not. -Irish

It is hard to live, but it is harder still to die. -Albanian

It is hard for a man who stands to talk to one who is seated. -Russian

When things go well it is easy to advise. -Dutch

Nothing is easy to the unwilling. -English

It is hard to pay for bread that has already been eaten. -Danish

No matter how hard you try the bull will never give milk. -Ukrainian

To promise is easy, to keep is troublesome. -Danish

It is hard to track the path the ship follows in the ocean. -Danish

Sloth makes all things difficult, but industry all things easy. -English

The thief has an easy job and bad dreams. -Yiddish

All things are difficult before they are easy. -English

It is not easy to show the way to a blind man. -Italian

It is easy to threaten a bull from a window. -Italian

He who throws himself under the
bench will be left to lie there. -Danish

He who spends a night
with a chicken will cackle
in the morning. -Tunisian

He who talks to a silent
listener will soon stand
naked. -Japanese

She who disappoints another is
unworthy to be trusted. -Yoruba

He who starts singing too high will
never finish the song. -German

She who could foresee affairs,
three days in advance would be rich
for thousands of years. -Chinese

She who deserves wine should
not be given water. -Ghanian

She who depends on another
dines ill and sups worse. -English

She who crosses the sea is wet. -Wolof

He who takes a light to find
a snake should start at
his own feet. -African

44

The eyes eat not but they know what will satisfy. -Fulani

If you speak with a cunning mouth, I listen with a cunning ear. -Annang

Ears are usually uninvited guests. -African

Taking aim for too long can ruin your eyes. -Ivorian

The stranger has big eyes but he doesn't see anything. -Ivorian

Distracted by what is far away, he does not see his nose. -Madagascan

The one-eyed man thanks God only when he sees
a man blind in both eyes. -Nigerian

Even the sharpest ear cannot hear an ant singing. -Sudanese

"Oh tongue, I am slapped for you," said the ear. -Oromo

Even if your eye dies, it still stays in your head. -Ghanian

If two wise people divide three eyes, it doesn't go well. -Ghanian

A messenger is the eye of his sender. -Lugbara

Being told is not adequate; I want to see with my eyes -Lugbara

Eyes don't steal another's things. -Oromo

The ears of a chief are as big as those of an elephant. -Ghanian

There is an opening in every ear, but some ears don't hear. -Ghanian

If your ear is stopped up, you clean it out with a stick,
you don't pierce it. -Ghanian

The blood of the one without ears will pour out. -Lugbara

Although one cries, the deaf person will not hear. -Oromo

A stranger may have very big eyes, but he doesn't see what is going on among
the people he is living with. -Ghanian

The blind are quick at hearing; the deaf are quick at sight. -Chinese

There is a big difference between what one hears and sees. -Japanese

Eyelashes, though near, are not seen. -Japanese

Fields have eyes, and the wilderness has ears. -Hindi

If you wish to know the mind of a man, listen to his words. -Chinese

Too much money blinds the eyes. -Lebanese

Instead of opening your mouth, open your eyes. -Turkish

I'm talking to the door, but I want the walls to hear me. -Afghan

Blind eyes see better than blind hearts. -Arabian

Nothing but a handful of dust will fill the eyes of man. -Arabian

A good orator makes us see with our ears. -Arabian

Words from the heart reach the heart, words from the mouth
reach the ear. -Arabian

Only through the eyes of others can we really see our own faults. -Chinese

Do something good and your neighbor will never know,
do something bad and they will hear about it a hundred miles away. -Chinese

If you enter the city of the blind, cover your eyes. -Iranian

Listen with one ear; be suspicious with the other. -Laotian

If you are too sparing with the cat's food, the rats will eat your ears. -Lebanese

The proportion of things thrill the eye. -Malaysian

There are men who walk through the woods and see no trees. -Mongolian

The eye never has enough of seeing, nor the ear its fill of hearing. -Biblical

A hungry belly has no ears. -French

The camel does not see his own hump. -Armenian

They who dance are thought mad by those who hear not the music. -English

Wide ears and a short tongue is best. -English

Abroad one has a hundred eyes, at home not one. -German

Eyes can see everything except themselves. -Serbo-Croatian

One eye of the master's sees more than ten of the servants'. -English

The eyes of the hare are not the same as the eyes of the owl. -Greek

What the eye doesn't see, the heart doesn't feel. -Yiddish

Do not blow
in the **bear's ear.** -Czech

Of money, wit, and virtue, believe one-fourth of what you hear. -English

In the eyes of the jealous a mushroom grows into a palm tree. -Russian

All men have three ears, one on the left of his head,
one on the right and one in his heart. -Armenian

Do not buy with your ears but with your eyes. -Czech

The back has to pay for what the ears didn't hear. -Finnish

You do not always have to believe what you see. -French

Never whisper to the deaf or wink at the blind. -Slovenian

The longer the blind live, the more they see. -Yiddish

Many people see things but few understand them. -Yiddish

The Tsar has three hands but only one ear. -Russian

By delaying, Orubadra lost
the head of his goat. -Lugbara

Compete—don't envy.
-Yemeni

Better a sound donkey than
a consumptive philosopher.
-Romanian

Beauty doesn't exist, men
only dream it. -Arabian

Cactus is bitter only to him
who tastes it. -Ethiopian

Beware of the goat that is in
the lion's lair. -Bambara

Better to write down something one
time than to read something ten times.
-Japanese

Children are equal to their parents, but the ears of the parents
are greater. -Oromo

Build a small house, and live thriftily.
-Tamil

Better a handful of dry dates
and content therewith than
to own the Gate of Peacocks
and be kicked in the eye by a
broody camel. -Arabian

A boulder is the father of rocks. -Yoruba

The calf is not afraid of the mother's horns. -African

There is no mother like your own mother. -Bambara

When you follow in the path of your father, you learn to walk like him.
-Ghanian

A mother's wrath does not survive the night. -Burundi

One father can feed seven children, but seven children
cannot feed one father. -Cameroonian

Every beetle is a gazelle in the eyes of its mother. -Moroccan

Except for my father and my mother everybody lies. -Berber

When the child falls the mother weeps; when the mother falls
the child laughs. -Swahili

A hundred aunts is not the same as one mother. -Sierra Leonean

They asked the mule who his father was. He said, "My uncle is the horse."
-Tunisian

If you have caught the mother hen, you pick up
her chicks without difficulty. -Ghanian

Even if your mother is not a good person, she is still your mother. -Ghanian

The earth is the mother of all. -Lugbara

A mother's breast goes dry but her hand does not. -Oromo

Before Father Ananse begot his son Ntikuma
he had someone to carry his money bag. -Ghanian

Nobody has two fathers. -Ghanian

The son whom they pampered, kills his father. -Oromo

A child who does not fear his father and mother will not live long. -Ovambo

The family that has peace when the father is there,
will have peace when the father is absent. -Oromo

The mother is to the child what the king is to the nation. -Vietnamese

The mother of someone who is killed can sleep; the mother
of the murderer cannot. -Arabian

The father in praising his son extolls himself. -Chinese

Whoever buys a house must examine the beams; whoever wants a wife
must look at her mother. -Chinese

Judge a man not by the words of his mother, but from
the comments of his neighbors. -Hebrew

Garlic is as good as ten mothers. -Indian

You only appreciate your father
the day you become a father yourself. -Iranian

To rear and not educate is the father's fault. -Chinese

The strictness of the teacher is better to bear
than the prejudice of the father. -Iranian

The goodness of the father reaches higher than a mountain; that of the
mother goes deeper than the ocean. -Japanese

You can buy everything, except a father and a mother. -Tamil

Even children of the same mother look different. -Korean

A child without a mother is like a fish in shallow water. -Burmese

If the father is a good man, the son will behave well. -Vietnamese

The talk of the child in the street is that of his father or his mother. -Hebrew

The value of father is known after his decease,
that of salt when exhausted. -Tamil

The young rely on their fathers, the old on their children. -Vietnamese

My fathers planted for me, and I planted for my children. -Hebrew

When the mother dies the father becomes an uncle. -Tamil

As a child, is a man wrapped in his mother's womb; as an adult,
in tradition; comes death, and he is wrapped in earth. -Malaysian

No bones are broken by a mother's fist. -Russian

Ask the mother if the child be like his father. -English

Better the child should cry than the father. -Yiddish

Whatever a child babbles, its mother will understand. -Yiddish

Time is the father of truth. -English

One cannot please everybody and one's father. -French

One father is more than a hundred schoolmasters. -English

The greatest love is mother-love; after that comes a dog's love; and after that the love of a sweetheart. -Polish

In the eyes of its mother every turkey is a **swan.** -Luxembourgian

Few are like father, no one is like mother. -Icelandic

An ounce of mother is worth a ton of priest. -Spanish

Practice is the mother of perfection. -Welsh

When a mother shouts at her child "Bastard," you can believe her. -Yiddish

Children suck the mother when they are young, and the father when they are old. -English

A father is a banker provided by nature. -French

As the field, so the crops; as the father, so the sons. -German

He goes safely to trial whose father is a judge. -Spanish

A child may have too much of his mother's blessing. -English

There is no grief greater than that of a mother. -Maltese

Everyone can keep house better than her mother till she tries. -English

He who smells does not know it himself. -Japanese

He who sows his grain in the field puts his trust in Heaven. -Chinese

She who does not punish evil invites it. -German

He who speaks the truth should have one foot in the stirrup. -Hindi

He who speaks a lot learns little. -Armenian

She who does not eat garlic does not smell of garlic. -Lebanese

She who does not have a chicken despises the goat of another. -Oromo

She who does not know is forgiven by God. -African

She who does not feed the dog feeds the thief. -Chinese

He who spares the rod hates his son, but he who loves him is careful to discipline him. -Biblical

By going and coming a bird weaves its nest. -Oji

A wax bullet is not used to shoot an elephant. -Ashanti

A baby chicken sleeps under a hawk's tree without knowing it. -Kpelle

The chicken is no match for the knife. -Swahili

A cow does not know the value of its tail until it is cut off. -Swahili

Two crocodiles do not live in one hole. -Ga

A dog lying down has surrendered. -Shona

Only a gadfly can sit on an elephant's back. -Hausa

A lizard suns itself within reach of its hiding place. -Shona

A hen does not play with a cat. -Fulani

When you see a monkey on a tree it has already seen you. -Fulani

An ostrich chick is too much for a hawk to pick up. -Hausa

Two birds disputed about a kernel, when a third swooped down and carried it off. -Congolese

The snake and the crab don't sleep in the same hole. -Congolese

Better half a donkey than half a camel. -Egyptian

A hawk doesn't swoop on a stone ball unless there's a piece of meat on it. -Hausa

The cattle is as good as the pasture in which it grazes. -Ethiopian

When spiders' webs unite, they can tie up a lion. -Ethiopian

A flea can trouble a lion more than the lion can harm a flea. -Kenyan

Ants can attack with a grain of rice. -Madagascan

53

An ant hole may collapse an embankment. -Japanese

A buffalo does not feel the weight of his own horns. -Hindi

The dog barks and the caravan passes on. -Turkish

Even an elephant may slip. -Tamil

A good man protects three villages; a good dog, three houses. -Chinese

Don't strike at fish in front of the trap. -Thai

A frog in the well knows not the ocean. -Japanese

Even a good horse cannot wear two saddles. -Chinese

Ivory does not grow in the mouth of a dog. -Chinese

Better to be eaten by a lion than to be eaten by a hyena. -Lebanese

When the tiger kills, the jackal profits. -Afghan

The mantis seizes the locust but does not see
the yellow bird behind him. -Chinese

The dreams of a cat are full of mice. -Arabian

To feed the ambition in your heart is like carrying a tiger under your arm.
-Chinese

You don't need a dog to catch a lame hare. -Chinese

Don't let the falcon loose until you see the hare. -Chinese

Four horses cannot overtake the tongue. -Chinese

To serve a prince is like sleeping with a tiger. -Chinese

It is no good going to the river just wanting to catch a fish; you have to take
a net as well. -Chinese

A tiger cannot beat a crowd of monkeys. -Chinese

An ant is over six feet tall when measured by its own foot-rule. -Slovenian

Asses carry the oats and horses eat them. -Dutch

Better an ass that carries me than a horse that throws me. -Portuguese

Every ass thinks himself worthy to stand with the king's horses. -English

A dead bee will make no honey. -English

Bees that have honey in their mouths have stings in their tails. -English

A bird may be caught with a snare that will not be shot. -English

A little bird is content with a little nest. -English

Every bird has a hawk above it. -Serbo-Croatian

The bear dances, but the gypsy takes the money. -Russian

A golden bit makes none the better horse. -Italian

The calf belongs to the owner of the cow. -Irish

A cat is a lion to a mouse. -Albanian

The cats that drive away mice are as good as those that catch them. -German

Who is born of a cat will run after mice. -French

A ragged colt may make a good horse. -English

A cow may be black, but her milk is white. -Serbo-Croatian

Better one cow in the stable than ten in the field. -Yiddish

The greatest crabs are not always the best meat. -English

Crows are never the whiter for washing themselves. -English

Crafty people do not share
the same bedroom. -Zulu

Don't look for speed in a
cheap horse; be content
if it neighs. -Nigerois

Don't look where you fell,
but where you slipped. -Liberian

Do not insult the river god
while crossing the river.
-Chinese

Don't draw a sword
against a louse. -Chinese

Destiny spoils plans. -Turkish

Do not tear down the east wall
to repair the west. -Chinese

Don't let an old person who is
dying curse you. -Oromo

Do not prophesy to the
man who can see further
than you can. -Japanese

Do not stand in a dangerous place
trusting in miracles. -Arabian

On a dead tree there are no monkeys. -Bantu

Fishing without a net is just bathing. -Nigerois

The bird flies high, but always returns to earth. -Nigerian

Until the lions have their historians,
tales of the hunt shall always glorify the hunter. -Nigerian

A tiger does not have to proclaim its tigritude. -Nigerian

Even though chickens don't wash, their eggs are still white. -Sierra Leonean

A roaring lion kills no game. -Ugandan

When the **ducks** are **quacking** the **frogs** take it as a **warning.**
-Madagascan

On the palm tree that yields nuts the birds will tarry. -Jabo

Nobody exchanges his eagle feathers for the feathers of a vulture. -Ghanian

The vulture doesn't have a good name and its body
doesn't have a good scent. -Ghanian

The vulture and raven have different destinies. -Ghanian

The fart of a baby elephant is never louder than its mother's. -Ghanian

Even if the elephant is thin, its meat will fill a hundred baskets. -Ghanian

After the elephant there is still a greater animal, the hunter! -Ghanian

Two small antelopes can beat one big antelope. -Ghanian

Regardless of its age the donkey will go eventually
into the stomach of the hyena. -Oromo

The donkey will not go with the hyena, the hen with the wolf,
nor the goat with the leopard. -Oromo

The hand can tame all the wild animals, even the hyena. -Oromo

The hyena said, "This meat is tasteless, tasteless,"
and it finished the whole donkey. -Oromo

Two dogs can kill a lion. -Hebrew

When an elephant is in trouble, even a frog will kick him. -Indian

The world flatters the elephant and tramples on the ant. -Indian

Every dog is a tiger in his own street. -Indian

In the end, all foxes meet at the furriers. -Indian

What is sport to the boy is the death of the bird. -Indian

Calm water does not mean there are no crocodiles. -Indonesian

Taking pity on a bloodthirsty panther does a great injustice to the sheep.
-Iranian

the For his master dog is a lion. -Iranian

A pig used to dirt turns its nose up at rice. -Japanese

You can't straighten a snake by putting it in a bamboo cane. -Japanese

The sparrow flying behind the hawk thinks the hawk is fleeing. -Japanese

Tigers die and leave their skins; people die and leave their names. -Japanese

In the valley where there are no tigers the hare is king. -Korean

Live with vultures, and become a vulture;
live with crows, and become a crow. -Laotian

One muddy buffalo makes the whole herd dirty. -Malaysian

The turtle lays thousands of eggs without anyone knowing, but when the
hen lays an egg, the whole country is informed. -Malaysian

A wolf will still be a wolf even if he hasn't eaten your sheep. -Manchurian

A donkey that carries me is worth more than a horse that kicks me.
-Mongolian

A tiger wearing a bell will starve. -Mongolian

The death of the wolf is the health of the sheep. -English

Little dogs start the hare but great ones catch it. -English

The smith's dog sleeps at the noise of the hammer
and wakes at the grinding of teeth. -Spanish

You cannot fly like an eagle with the wings of a wren. -English

Fish look for deeper waters and men for where it's better. -Russian

There are as good fish in the sea as ever came out of it. -English

It is a poor fox that has but one hole. -German

Roast geese don't come flying into your mouth. -Dutch

A fly can drive away **horses.** -Greek

In every man's heart there is a sleeping lion. -Armenian

It is no honor for an eagle to vanquish a dove. -Italian

A horse has four legs and even he stumbles. -Russian

A man, a horse, and a dog are never weary of each other's company. -English

Don't drive the horse with a whip, but with oats. -Russian

One can't shoe a running horse. -Dutch

You ride as you like on your own horse. -Russian

Kings and bears often worry their keepers. -English

What the lion cannot, the fox can. -German

A man is a lion in his own cause. -English

If men become sheep, the wolf will devour them. -English

He who slaps himself on the face
should not cry ouch. -Lebanese

He who rents one garden will
eat birds; who rents gardens,
the birds will eat him. -Hebrew

She who drinks a little too
much drinks much too much.
-German

He who serves two masters has
to lie to one. -Portuguese

He who restrains his impatience to eat will find his food
the sweeter. -Hausa

She who does not rise
early never does a good
day's work. -English

She who does not speak does not argue.
-Ovambo

She who doesn't scatter the
morning dew will not comb
gray hairs. -Irish

She who does not recognize a hint, will
not understand even if told. -Oromo

He who rides upon an ass
cannot help but smell its gas!
-African

The hyena will not enter the hole of the anteater. -Oromo

They do not cut tusks from the living elephant. -Oromo

The hawk does not fly until its wings reach full strength. -Oromo

The goat dwells among men for fear of the leopard. -Jabo

As long as the mouse keeps still you can be sure that
the cat stays on guard. -Madagascan

When children see an eagle that has been beaten by the rain,
they say it is a vulture. -Ghanian

Even if the forest is undone, the elephant is above running. -Hausa

The hare said, "I am swift,"
the plateau said, "I am vast."
-Basotho

The lion is the pet of the forest: let every beast take heed how he feeds,
for the lion does not eat stale meat. -Yoruba

When all the animals show their beauty,
the leopard is chosen as the most beautiful one. -Ghanian

"A handsome one without a fault!" said the hyena
looking at itself in the glass. -Oromo

No matter how much the world changes, cats will never lay eggs. -Bambara

A small bee stung an elephant fatally. -Lugbara

The horse only brings to the war, it does not fight. -Oromo

Even if the mouse were the size of a cow, he would be
the cat's slave nevertheless. -Ashanti

No one should ask the fish what happens in the plain;
nor should the rat be asked what takes place in the water. -Yoruba

However poor the elephant, it will be worth more than ten frogs. -Hausa

The flight of the eagle will not stop that of the sand fly. -Fulani

A man may be as strong as the buffalo, yet he has no horns. -Yoruba

When you treat someone like a wild cat, he will steal your chickens. -Madagascan

A man with little learning is like the frog who thinks
its pond is an ocean. -Burmese

A good tree can lodge ten thousand birds. -Burmese

One arrow does not bring down two birds. -Turkish

It is no disgrace to move out of the way of the elephant. -Vietnamese

The sluggard says, "There is a lion in the road,
a fierce lion roaming the streets!" -Biblical

By the continual creeping of ants a stone will wear away. -Tamil

Tiger and deer do not walk together. -Chinese

Don't climb a tree to look for fish. -Chinese

Soft words will get the snake out of its hole.
-Iranian

A cat is a lion in a jungle of small bushes. -Hindi

Small cats catch small mice. -Vietnamese

When the snake is old, the frog will tease him. -Iranian

A chicken you eat only once—eggs a hundred times. -Tajik

You can't catch two frogs with one hand. -Chinese

If a rat wants to die it bites a cat's tail. -Chinese

The summer insect cannot talk of ice; the frog in the well
cannot talk of Heaven. -Chinese

It is better to go home and make your net than to gaze
longingly at the fish in the deep pool. -Japanese

A blind cat catches only a dead rat. -Chinese

If you live on the river, befriend the crocodile. -Iranian

You cannot cook one half of the chicken and have the other lay eggs.
-Sanskrit

A monkey remains a monkey, though dressed in silk. -Spanish

Nature draws stronger than seven oxen. -German

The wolf loves the fog. -Albanian

The wolf and the dog agree about the goat—which together they eat. -Basque

Choosy pigs never get fat. -French

Don't slaughter more pigs than you can salt. -French

Mules make a great fuss about their ancestors having been donkeys. -German

The frog wanted to be an ox and swelled up until he burst. -Greek

A good cat deserves a good rat. -French

Ill-matched horses draw badly. -Dutch

When the shepherd strays, the sheep stray. -Dutch

It is the quiet pigs that eat the meal. -Irish

What does a donkey know about the life of a nightingale? -Romanian

Though you seat the frog on a golden stool, he'll soon jump off it into the pool. -German

Rotten straw can harm a healthy horse. -Russian

The advice of foxes is dangerous for chickens. -Spanish

Fat geese don't fly far. -Walloon

An old wolf is used to being shouted at. -Dutch

The eagle does not wage war against frogs. -Italian

A donkey is asked to a wedding either to carry water or to bring wood.
-Greek

Even if the whole world con-
spired against you—that would
not inflict a quarter of the harm
you inflict yourself. -Turkish

Every excuse is good,
if it works. -Italian

Even in the freshest of milk,
you will still find hairs. -Bambara

Don't stop sowing just because
the birds ate a few seeds. -Danish

Even dust, if amassed
enough, will form a great
mountain. -Korean

Everyone thinks his own spit
tastes good. -Iranian

Even a thief takes ten years
to learn his trade. -Japanese

Even a fool can govern if
nothing happens. -German

Eat bad soup with a big spoon. -Armenian

Even if the old woman has no
teeth, her tiger nuts remain in
her own bag. -Ghanian

A mother that has lost many children by death, hates the idea of her child taking a nap. -Annang

Whoever lets himself be led by the heart will never lose his way. -Egyptian

When he looked under the saddle he lost his horse. -Ethiopian

What comes out of the mouth has lost its master. -Gabonese

Desperate search doesn't cause finding. -Hausa

The one who keeps asking doesn't lose the way. -Ghanian

A camel that was lost in the morning is not found in the evening. -Oromo

A blind man does not worry over the loss of a looking glass. -Hausa

Even in the dark, the hand will find the mouth. -Oromo

The one who is weak in shepherding will be strong in searching. -Oromo

If you allow your emotions to rule you, you are lost. -Ghanian

If a string of beads break in the presence of elders, they are not lost. -Ghanian

A big thing does not get lost. -Ghanian

Because he lost his reputation he lost a kingdom. -Oromo

In order to find evildoers, every human being is given a name. -Ghanian

If the nose finds something, the eye also finds it. -Ghanian

In order to find what we need when we want it, we put it together in a bundle. -Ghanian

If you trample on another person's things in looking for your own, you never find them. -Ghanian

They search even in the pounding mortar for the lost camel. -Oromo

Those which are useful cannot be easily found. -Basotho

65

At steady gambling even the gods and immortals lose. -Chinese

One who has nothing to lose can be reckless to any extent. -Bihar

Once you have found your rhythm, you will then know your God. -Arabian

There's many a good man to be found under a shabby hat. -Chinese

Win a cat and lose a cow—the consequence of litigation. -Chinese

While wrangling over a quarter of pig,
you can lose a flock of sheep. -Chinese

The pleasure of finding something is worth more
than what you find. -Iranian

Bald people can always find a comb. -Thai

While yearning for excess we lose the necessities. -Iranian

When a king is about to lose his power
his orders burn more intensely than fire. -Tibetan

If a thief finds nothing to steal, he thinks himself honest. -Hebrew

Beauty is found only in one of a thousand. -Tamil

A lost inch of gold may be found; a lost inch of time, never. -Chinese

A camel with bells is not lost. -Turkish

If you lose your needle in the grass, look for it in the grass. -Chinese

Easily had opportunities are easily lost. -Japanese

Don't let high waves scare you to lose the oars. -Vietnamese

If you find honey, eat just enough—
too much of it, and you will vomit. -Biblical

For finding happiness one must walk till he be wearied. -Turkish

Once a horse is born, someone will be found to ride it. -Hebrew

Better lose the anchor than the whole ship. -Dutch

In a good apple you sometimes find a worm. -Yiddish

There is no beard so well shaven but another barber will find something more to shave from it. -Italian

You must lose a fly to catch a trout. -English

First find the ford, then cross the river. -Armenian

Sometimes the best gain is to lose. -English

A greyhound finds its food in its feet. -Irish

The timid man loses many good things. -Greek

It is lost that is unsought. -English

A man must take such as he finds, or such as he brings. -English

When the sea turned into honey, the beggar lost his spoon. -Bulgarian

Better ask twice than to lose your way once. -Danish

If the bread in the oven is a failure you lose a week; if the harvest is a failure you lose a year; if marriage is a failure then you lose a life. -Estonian

There is no old bread that cannot find its cheese. -French

All the treasures of the earth can't bring back one lost moment. -French

If you lend something you may lose it, but not if you give it. -French

Who seeks a quarrel will find it near at hand. -Italian

Under a tattered cloak you will generally find a good drinker. -Spanish

Don't cross the stream to find water. -Swedish

At the bottom of the sack you will find the bill. -Swiss

67

She who eats cheese finds
water. -Turkish

He who plunders with a little boat is a pirate;
he who plunders with a fleet is a conqueror. -Greek

She who follows the crowd
has many companions. -German

He who refuses a gift will
not fill his barn. -Sierra Leonean

He who prays for his neighbors will be
heard for himself. -Hebrew

She who fetches water
breaks the pot. -Oji

She who fears to suffer,
suffers from fear. -French

She who flatters me is my enemy, who
blames me is my teacher. -Chinese

He who refuses the advice of a person will
take the advice of Satan. -Oromo

He who recognizes his folly is on
the road to wisdom. -Norwegian

A distant fire does not burn. -Swahili

Fire and gunpowder do not sleep together. -Ashanti

Put out the fire while it is small. -Hausa

The fire which is screened by elders is not dangerous. -Bemba

Where water is the boss, there must the land obey. -African

The only insurance against fire is to have two houses. -Nigerois

A piece of wood that has been burned easily catches fire. -Togolese

Clouds do not always mean rain, but smoke is a sure sign of fire. -African

Water doesn't refuse to go down, nor smoke to go up. -Madagascan

You cannot do without water, even if it drowned your child. -Ovambo

The crocodile lies in the water, but it breathes the air. -Ghanian

An idea is like running water. -Ghanian

If plain water was satisfying enough,
then the fish would not take the hook. -Ghanian

Because the water has dried up in the river,
the eagle is catching the fish. -Ghanian

If you are patient and wait till the water becomes clear, you will find what you
are looking for at the bottom of the water. -Ghanian

He dug a well to fetch water. -Ghanian

A fire goes out only when firewood is withheld. -Oromo

Big talk: it's head is fire, it's behind is water. -Oromo

Fire and an adversary are not to be trusted. -Oromo

The fool thirsts standing in water. -Oromo

69

Cotton cannot play with fire. -Turkish

A crocodile cares not whether the water is deep or shallow. -Tamil

The elephant and tiger are afraid of fire. -Tamil

Strike a flint and you get fire;
don't strike it and not even smoke will come. -Chinese

The flow of water and the future of human beings are uncertain. -Japanese

Fuel alone will not light a fire. -Chinese

After a house is burnt, one becomes cautious of fire. -Korean

When men are really friends, then even water is sweet. -Chinese

Don't use oiled paper to wrap up fire. -Chinese

Fire makes mud hard and gold melt. -Chinese

The greatest virtue is like water; good for everything. -Chinese

Water can do without fishes, fishes cannot do without water. -Chinese

Flowing water never gets dirty. -Chinese

Water from far away is no good for a fire close by. -Chinese

If you are in a boat you are more afraid of fire
than you are of water. -Japanese

Water will always take the form of the vase it fills. -Japanese

Even foul water will quench fire. -Mongolian

Water may flow in a thousand channels, but it all returns to the sea. -Chinese

With one stump you can't make a good fire. -Thai

Water can support a ship, and water can upset it. -Chinese

Little chips kindle the fire, and big logs sustain it. -Portuguese

Beware of a silent dog and a still water. -English

The water in which one drowns is always an ocean. -Armenian

Drops of water eat up stones. -Greek

If one is fated to drown, he will drown in a spoonful of water. -Yiddish

By labor fire is got out of a stone. -Dutch

Fire in the heart sends smoke into the head. -German

Fire, water, and governments don't understand mercy. -Albanian

Water is the strongest drink; **it drives mills.** -German

He that will have fire must bear with smoke. -Dutch

Kindle not a fire that you cannot extinguish. -English

The dog does not know how to swim until the water reaches his ears. -Russian

God will cook the soup for him who has water, herbs, and wood. -Russian

When God wishes, even water can burn. -Russian

You cannot put a fire out with spit. -Armenian

Extol the virtue of water, but drink wine. -Czech

Better a small fire that warms you than a big one that burns you. -French

Fire does not extinguish fire. -Greek

Water never loses its way. -Russian

A hidden fire is discovered by its smoke. -Spanish

Go home when the table is set
and to church when the service
is almost over. -Armenian

Go and wake up your luck. -Iranian

Follow the advice of the one who
makes you cry, not from the one
who makes you laugh. -Arabian

God hears things upside down. -Lebanese

Give me, mother, luck at my
birth, then throw me if you will
on the rubbish heap. -Bulgarian

Fuel is not sold in the forest, nor
fish on the shore of a lake. -Chinese

For the disease of stubbornness
there is no cure. -Yiddish

Everything is small at the beginning and then grows; except
trouble, which is big at the beginning and still grows. -Arabian

From the roof of a house a melon
may roll either of two ways. -Chinese

From all the fish in the pot you can
only make one soup. -Madagascan

When there is nothing to eat but corn, rice is a luxury. -Hausa

Eat whatever you like, but dress as others do. -Egyptian

Famine compels one to eat the fruit of all kinds of trees. -Yoruba

Nobody cooks food and places it in the road to seek a guest. -Oji

Even the best cooking pot will not produce food. -African

If you are looking for a fly in your food it means that you are full. -South African

If you watch your pot, your food will not burn. -Mauritanian

A rotten fish pollutes the whole kitchen. -Wolof

There is no god like one's stomach; we must sacrifice to it every day. -Yoruba

A soup that tastes good by licking must taste better by eating. -Annang

The person doomed to the crocodile
spends too much time drinking at the river. -Oromo

Only the truth satisfies, not drink. -Oromo

If someone loves you, he invites you for a drink. -Ghanian

No one leaves a flowing river to go to drink from a pool. -Ghanian

Because of the future and out of respect for a person,
one drinks the last bit of palm wine from the calabash. -Ghanian

When water is drowning you, you drink some of it. -Ghanian

No matter how thirsty one becomes, one cannot drink dry the river. -Oromo

Once you have drunk the dregs of palm wine, it delivers a message. -Ghanian

If you have a mouth, get some palm wine! -Ghanian

When a person drinks palm wine he doesn't remain quiet. -Ghanian

73

Friends and wine, the older the better. -Japanese

A red-nosed man may not be a drunkard,
but he will always be called one. -Chinese

You won't gain knowledge by drinking ink. -Arabian

To stop drinking, study a drunkard when you are sober. -Chinese

All rotten fish taste the same. -Chinese

A lot of people become saints because of their stomach. -Indian

Who has not had a taste longs to do so, but for whom has tasted,
then the longing is a hundred times more. -Iranian

First the man takes a drink; then the drink takes a drink;
after that the drink takes the man. -Japanese

At high tide fish eat ants;
at low tide ants eat fish. -Thai

No matter if you eat a little or a lot of garlic,
the smell is just as strong. -Tibetan

If the master gets drunk it is an honorable drunkenness;
if the servant does it is evidence of his mean disposition. -Tibetan

The first drink makes you a frisky gazelle,
the second an impetuous zebra, the third a roaring lion,
and with the fourth you become a silly donkey. -Turkish

The famished person is not choosy about his food. -Japanese

The tastes of ten people differ as ten colors. -Japanese

Wine begins with formalities and ends in a riot. -Japanese

Wine is the best of all medicines and the worst of all poisons. -Japanese

How can one start a fast with baklava in one's hand. -Armenian

Until your fortieth it is better to eat than to drink;
afterwards it is vice versa. -Hebrew

Eat according to the limits of your provisions;
walk according to the length of your step. -Tibetan

If you want your dinner, don't offend the cook. -Chinese

What you do when you're drunk you must pay for when you're dry. -Scottish

If you drink you die, if you don't drink you die,
so it is better to drink. -Russian

A drunk can sleep it off, but never a fool. -Russian

Eat until you are half satisfied, and drink until you are half drunk. -Russian

If fools ate no bread, corn would be cheap. -Dutch

A hungry man smells meat afar off. -English

A drunkard can be a sheep, a monkey or a lion. -Danish

Eat with pleasure;
drink with measure. -French

What the sober man has in his heart, the drunkard has on his lips. -Danish

Don't dig your grave with your own knife and fork. -English

Where love sets the table food tastes at its best. -French

The torch of love is lit in the kitchen. -French

If the wine bothers you while you work, stop working. -French

More people drown in glasses than in rivers. -German

Adam ate the apple, and our teeth still ache. -Hungarian

Even if a chef cooks just a fly, he would keep the breast for himself. -Polish

The first drink with water, the second without water,
the third like water. -Spanish

No cook ever died of starvation. -Ukrainian

One may tire of eating tarts. -French

75

Free vinegar tastes better than bought honey. -Albanian

He who plies many trades remains
without a house. -Greek

He who marries a young
woman gets welfare and a
treasure. -Moroccan

She who has a fever is not shown
to the fire. -Zambian

He who mixes himself with
the draff will be eaten by the
swine. -Dutch

He who pays no heed to the
words of his elders mounts
a wild horse. -Turkish

She who gets blisters from the hoe
handle will not die of hunger. -Swahili

She who gives a monkey as a present
doesn't keep hold of its tail. -Ivorian

She who gets stuck on
petty happiness will not
attain great happiness.
-Tibetan

She who hankers after praise
should move on. -Iranian

He who offers his back should
not complain if it is beaten. -Russian

A close friend can become a close enemy. -Ethiopian

The heart that does not decide is an enemy of its master. -Oromo

Bribery is the enemy of justice. -Swahili

Gossiping about the enemy brings war. -Jabo

The enemy of a chief is he who has grown up
with him from childhood. -Ashanti

Your enemy will not praise you, even though you catch
a leopard and give it to him. -Hausa

If you make friends on the road, your knife will be lost. -Oji

Hold a true friend with both your hands. -Kanuri

If the hare is your enemy, admit that he can run fast. -Bambara

Pass by your enemy hungry but never naked. -Egyptian

A powerful friend becomes a powerful enemy. -Ethiopian

Reinforcement beats the foe. -Oji

One man's enemy is another man's friend. -Ghanian

If your enemy is in trouble, help him, but if he thanks you, don't reply. -Ghanian

A brother who is an enemy to his brother is like fire in the underwear. -Oromo

When your enemy imitates your dancing,
he twists his hips in an awkward manner. -Ghanian

When a man is born, his enemy is also born. -Ghanian

When there is no enemy within, the enemies outside cannot hurt you. -African

Those who suspect each other cannot
watch together for their common enemy. -Oromo

A day with your friend is better than a year with one who hates you. -Hausa

Beware, the enemy lies under your blanket. -Indonesian

Do not sigh, for your enemy will hear and rejoice. -Yemeni

The fox's enemy is its tail. -Tajik

When your enemies attack, bathe in their blood. -Islamic

An enemy's envy is his own punishment. -Tamil

Carelessness is a great enemy. -Japanese

Make no one an enemy without cause. -Turkish

Better a thousand enemies outside the tent than one within. -Arabian

Your friend will swallow your mistakes,
your enemy will present them on a plate. -Arabian

Who is mighty?
One who makes
an enemy
into a friend. -Hebrew

Don't trust the smile of your opponent. -Babylonian

If thine enemy wrong thee, buy each of his children a drum. -Chinese

It is a real compliment that comes from an enemy. -Iranian

There are three kinds of enemy: the enemy himself, the friends of your
enemy, and the enemies of your friends. -Iranian

Use your enemy's hand to catch a snake. -Iranian

The store of rice in your attic is your enemy—
it makes them who have none very jealous. -Thai

One good punch on your enemy's nose, gives more pleasure than hearing
well-meaning advice from your elders. -Tibetan

Be thine enemy an ant, see in him an elephant. -Turkish

Care for your horse as a friend; ride it as if it were an enemy. -Turkish

A weapon is an enemy even to its owner. -Turkish

Better have a dog for your friend than your enemy. -Dutch

An enemy may chance to give good counsel. -English

One old friend is better than two new ones. -Russian

It's easy to acquire an enemy; hard to acquire a friend. -Yiddish

There is no such thing as an insignificant enemy. -French

When your enemy falls, don't rejoice; but don't pick him up either. -Yiddish

Your enemy makes you wise. -Italian

A friend's fault should be known but not abhorred. -Portuguese

When your enemy retreats, **make him a golden bridge.** -Dutch

A friend is not so soon gotten as lost. -English

A friend who leads one astray is an enemy. -Greek

Blessed is the man who has friends, but woe to him who needs them. -Czech

Real friends will share even a strawberry. -Slovakian

The friend that can be bought is not worth buying. -Irish

If we are bound to forgive an enemy, we are not bound to trust him. -English

When a friend asks there is no tomorrow. -English

One God, one wife, but many friends. -Dutch

You do not know who is your friend or who is your enemy until the ice breaks. -Icelandic

The man who controls his wrath conquers his foe. -Greek

Many a friend has been lost by a jest, but none has ever been got by one. -Czech

God save you from a bad
neighbor, and from a begin-
ner on the fiddle. -Italian

He to whom things are
brought does not know the
length of the road. -Ovambo

He that measures oil shall
anoint his fingers. -English

He became an infidel hesitating
between two mosques. -Turkish

Happiness is not a horse, you
cannot harness it. -Russian

God made low branches for birds
that cannot fly so well. -Turkish

Have you ever seen the stars
coming down to the sea to ask
when it will rain? -Ghanian

Happiness is guarded
by bold warriors. -Hindi

Good counsel is no better
than bad counsel if it be not
taken in time. -Danish

Greet everyone cordially
when you don't know who
your in-laws are going to be.
-Madagascan

If you find a leopard in your house, make him your friend. -Swahili

Return to old watering holes for more than water;
friends and dreams are there to meet you. -African

Your friend chooses pebbles for you
and your enemy counts your faults. -Egyptian

A small house can lodge a hundred friends. -Egyptian

An onion shared with a friend tastes like roast lamb. -Egyptian

Bad friends prevent you from having good friends. -Gabonese

Friendship reminds us of fathers, love of mothers. -Madagascan

Sorrow is like a precious treasure, shown only to friends. -Madagascan

A friendly person is never a good-for-nothing. -Nigerian

An intelligent enemy is better than a stupid friend. -Wolof

A stone from the hand of a friend is an apple. -Moroccan

It is because of playing with friends that the crab has no head. -Ghanian

A friend of a thief is also a thief. -Basotho

Anger with our friend, rather than
constant friendship with our enemy. -Egyptian

At the narrow passage there is no brother and no friend. -Egyptian

Better lose a little money than a little friendship. -Madagascan

The first condition of friendship is to agree with each other. -Egyptian

The friend of a quarrel-picker is quarrelsome. -Ovambo

The hunger of your friend does not hinder sleep. -Bemba

When three of your enemies go aside to deliberate on the verdict
to be given you, who is going to find you innocent? -Ghanian

81

The pretty woman in the house is the enemy of all the ugly ones. -Chinese

Even though you become the enemy of a good man,
don't become the friend of a bad man. -Japanese

Eat and drink with a friend,
but have no business transaction with him. -Turkish

If friends have faith in each other,
life and death are of no consequence. -Chinese

It is difficult to win a friend in a year;
it is easy to offend one in an hour.
-Chinese

The friendship of two depends on the forbearance of one. -Tamil

Do not remove a fly from your friend's forehead with a hatchet. -Chinese

Make friends with what is good in a man and not his goods. -Chinese

When you have an ass for a friend, expect nothing but kicks. -Indian

Over-intelligent people can't find friends. -Japanese

No road is too long in the company of a friend. -Japanese

The winner has many friends, the loser has good friends. -Mongolian

None is so rich as that he can throw away a friend. -Turkish

Who seeks a faultless friend remains friendless. -Turkish

Wounds from a friend can be trusted, but an enemy multiplies kisses. -Biblical

An old friend is like a saddled horse. -Pashtun

As water lends itself to the shape of the vessel which contains it,
so a man is influenced by his good or bad friends. -Japanese

Build a fence even between intimate friends. -Japanese

Every rose has a thorn as its friend. -Pashtun

Mutual confidence is the pillar of friendship. -Chinese

Do not protect yourself by a fence, but rather by your friends. -Czech

Friendship is a plant we must often water. -German

One who seeks no friends is his own enemy. -Russian

A thousand friends are few; one enemy is too many. -Russian

Be slow in choosing a friend, but slower in changing him. -Scottish

An ounce of blood is worth more than a pound of friendship. -Spanish

See to it that you have many books and many friends—
but be sure they are good ones. -Spanish

If your enemy is up to his waist in water, give him your hand;
if the water reaches his shoulders, stand on his head. -Spanish

An enemy will agree, but a friend will argue.
-Russian

A friend to everybody and to nobody is the same thing. -Spanish

To see a friend no road is too long. -Ukrainian

Never trust overmuch to a new friend or an old enemy. -Welsh

What a man thinks up for himself,
his worst enemy couldn't wish for him. -Yiddish

In the mirror everybody sees his best friend. -Yiddish

You don't need to have one hundred rubles
if you have one hundred friends. -Russian

Do not spread your corn to dry at an enemy's door. -Spanish

An enemy does not sleep. -French

He cannot be a friend to any one who is his own enemy. -French

Every man will shoot at the enemy, but few will gather the shafts. -English

A secret is a friend; an enemy if you confide it. -Russian

She who has been bitten by a snake
fears a piece of string. -Iranian

He who lost his faith,
has nothing more to lose. -Spanish

She who has bad breath cannot smell it. -Ovambo

She who has health has hope, and she
who has hope has every thing. -Arabian

She who has a straw tail is always in
fear of its catching fire. -Italian

He who marries a beauty
marries trouble. -Nigerois

He who loves thinks that the
others are blind; the others
think that he is crazy. -Arabian

He who makes himself a dove
is eaten by the hawk. -Italian

He who loves peace minds his
own business. -Chinese

She who has a true friend, has
no need of a mirror. -Indian

A riddle made by God has no solution. -Zambian

Do not blame God for having created the tiger, but thank Him for not giving it wings. -Ethiopian

God speaks a foreign tongue. -Ovambo

If God has not decreed your death, and a human being tries to kill you, you will not die. -Ghanian

If you have forgotten God, you have forgotten yourself. -Swahili

It is impossible to bend the arm of God. -Masai

The chick loved by God will grow up, though motherless. -Hausa

If God were not forgiving, heaven would be empty. -Berber

What God sends you cannot send back. -Ganda

What is hidden to human beings is plain before God. -Yoruba

A flatterer is worse than the devil. -Ghanian

A thought that is bad is an egg of Satan. -Oromo

Evil enters like a needle and spreads like an oak tree. -Ethiopian

Hastiness is the work of the devil. -Oromo

It is the heart that carries one to hell or to heaven. -Kanuri

There are no fans in hell. -Egyptian

What the devil does in a year an old woman does in an hour. -Moroccan

When the angels present themselves, the devils abscond. -Egyptian

Woman conquers the devil. -Moroccan

Women are the snares of the devil. -Moroccan

Give to Caesar what is Caesar's, and to God what is God's. -Biblical

God seizes late, but seizes harshly. -Iranian

Make do with bread and butter until God can bring you jam. -Arabian

Man has a thousand schemes; Heaven has but one. -Chinese

The distance between heaven and earth is no greater than one thought.
-Mongolian

To follow the will of Heaven is to prosper; to rebel against the will of
Heaven is to be destroyed. -Chinese

When God shuts one door, He opens another. -Arabian

When God wishes a man well, He gives him insight into his faults. -Islamic

Trust in God, but tie your camel. -Iranian

Goodness speaks in a whisper, evil shouts. -Tibetan

A house without a woman is the devil's own lodging. -Indian

A polite devil is more agreeable than a rude saint. -Lebanese

Even the devil sometimes breaks his horns. -Japanese

If you really have to sin, then choose a sin that you enjoy. -Iranian

It is better to go hungry with a pure mind than to eat well with an evil one.
-Chinese

Suspicion generates dark devils. -Japanese

The devil will not bother you in a house full of children. -Kurdish

There is no saint without a past and no sinner without a future. -Iranian

When you talk about future happenings the devil starts to laugh. -Japanese

You don't have to die: heaven and hell are in this world too. -Japanese

All are not saints who go to church. -Italian

God does not bargain and God does not change. -Yiddish

God feeds the birds that use their wings. -Danish

God grant me a good sword and no use for it. -Polish

God often visits us, but most of the time we are not at home. -French

If God wills, even a cock will lay an egg. -Polish

Lend to God and the earth—they both pay good interest. -Swedish

Man does what he can and God what He will. -English

the Only God helps the badly dressed. -Spanish

A beautiful woman is paradise for the eye, the soul's hell,
and purgatory for the purse. -Estonian

It is better to visit hell in your lifetime than after you're dead. -Spanish

Everyone has his own devil, and some have two. -Swedish

If you do good to the Devil, out of gratitude he will deliver you to hell. -Czech

If you want to annoy the devil stay silent. -Bulgarian

It is harder work getting to hell than to heaven. -German

One man laughs at another, and the devil at all. -Romanian

The devil sometimes speaks the truth. -English

When the devil finds the door shut he goes away. -French

When the devil reigns today God will be master tomorrow. -German

Pray to God but continue to row to the shore. -Russian

I have a cow in the sky,
but cannot drink her milk.
-Ethiopian

If a stone falls on an egg, it is
bad for the egg; if an egg falls
onto a stone, it is still bad for
the egg. -Turkish

He who is master of his thirst is
master of his health. -French

However rich a man is, it is
not right to plunder his things
with big pans. -Ghanian

Hussars pray for war and
doctors for fever. -German

He who walks through a
field of onions, will smell
like an onion. -Arabian

If a centipede loses a leg,
it can still walk. -Burmese

However poor the crocodile becomes, it searches for food in the
river, not in the forest. -Ghanian

Hobby horses are more
expensive than Arabian
stallions. -German

Horse and cow face the
wind differently. -Chinese

Fingers which catch dirty things can be washed. -Bemba

A fugitive never stops to pick the thorns from his foot. -Yoruba

Be it ever so dark the hand will not miss the mouth. -Fulani

Without fingers the hand would be a spoon. -Wolof

If a child washes his hands he could eat with kings. -African

The fire cannot be put out with your hands. -Cameroonian

You cannot climb a tree with one hand. -Gabonese

Practice with the left hand while the right is still there. -African

You can catch a cricket in your hand
but its song is all over the field. -Madagascan

Be like the mouth and the hand: when the hand is hurt the mouth
blows on it, when the mouth is hurt the hand rubs it. -Madagascan

With shoes one can get on in the midst of thorns. -Yoruba

Many hands catch even a strong person. -Ghanian

If feet play with feet, there is no discord, but if mouth plays
with mouth there is discord. -Ghanian

A face which is not beautiful is like the sole of a person's foot. -Ghanian

If your hands are dirty, they are not as dirty as the soles of your feet. -Ghanian

A girl who is beautiful can be recognized by the heels of her feet. -Oromo

He gave it by hand and went after it by foot. -Oromo

The feet take a person to where one's heart is. -Oromo

The horseback rider does not know what the person on foot needs. -Oromo

The pinch from the shoe is felt by the foot. -Basotho

89

The axe well familiar to oneself may be wielded on one's own foot. -Korean

A bird is not taken with the hand. -Turkish

He lifts his feet high who puts on boots for the first time. -Chinese

A dry finger cannot take up salt. -Chinese

Though the left hand conquer the right, no advantage is gained. -Chinese

When the hands are many, they can break down the stoutest of walls.
-Hebrew

With bare hands one establishes a family fortune. -Korean

You can't pick up two melons with one hand. -Iranian

Don't use your teeth when you can untie the knot with your fingers. -Afghan

A cool head and warm feet are the cause of long life.
-Japanese

To make good conversation there are a thousand subjects, but there are still those who cannot meet a cripple without talking about feet. -Chinese

If you walk on snow you cannot hide your footprints. -Chinese

You can't look at the stars while you are walking if you have a stone in your shoe. -Chinese

The eyes can do a thousand things that the fingers can't. -Iranian

A gentle hand may lead even an elephant by a single hair. -Iranian

Don't scratch your shoe when it's your foot that itches. -Japanese

The turtle underestimates the value of fast feet. -Japanese

If you kick a stone in anger, you'll hurt your own foot. -Korean

When one's shoes are tight the world becomes tight on one's head. -Turkish

The tool works, the hand boasts. -Turkish

A baby is born with clenched fists
and a man dies with his hands open. -Yiddish

Better a crease in the shoe than a blister on the toe. -Estonian

If you can plug a hole with a finger, don't use your palm. -Slovakian

One foot is better than two crutches. -English

A hand in the water feels no pity for a hand in the fire. -Maltese

Dirty hands make clean money. -English

One hand washes the other, and both the face. -English

The right hand itches to get money, the left hand to spend it. -Russian

Where there is no head, woe to the feet. -Romanian

When your hand is in the dog's mouth withdraw it gently. -Irish

Industry is fortune's right hand and frugality her left. -English

You give money with your hand, but you go after it with your feet. -Russian

When the master hurts his foot the servants limp. -Danish

A beggar on his feet is worth more than an emperor in his grave. -French

Between saying and doing many a pair of shoes is worn out. -French

Who bathes his hands in blood will have to wash them with tears. -German

It is better to wear out one's shoes than one's sheets. -Italian

The same shoe does not fit every foot. -Italian

Who has not a good tongue, ought to have good hands. -English

Vengeance, though it comes with leaden feet,
strikes with iron hands. -English

He who looks on knows
more of the game than
he who plays. -German

She who has no power
depends on the one who
has. -Ghanian

He who lies in the sty will be
eaten by the pigs. -Yiddish

She who has no intelligence is
happy with it. -South African

She who has many irons
in the fire will let some of
them burn. -Danish

He who longs too much for
a child will marry a pregnant
woman. -Bambara

He who looks only at
heaven may easily break
his nose on earth. -Czech

She who has no care for
the far future will have
sorrow in the near future.
-Korean

He who lies under the table
gets kicked. -Polish

She who has nothing
is afraid of nothing.
-Portuguese

The end of the journey is reached by moving ahead. -Ovambo

If you are not inside a house, you do not know about its leaking. -Kpelle

Every journey gives you its own flavor. -Libyan

The laughter of a child is the light of a house. -Swahili

The leaf of a tree does not speak, nor does the road
tell the traveler what lies ahead. -Ovambo

Treat your guest as a guest for two days—
then on the third day give him a hoe. -African

The wise traveler leaves his heart at home. -African

The eye of the guest sees cockroaches giving birth.
-Oromo

The hare and the elephant don't travel well together. -Bambara

A house with two keys is worth nothing. -Congolese

Don't expect to be offered a chair when you visit a place where
the chief himself sits on the floor. -Ghanian

Affairs of the home should not be discussed in the public square. -Kenyan

It is not the fire in the fireplace which warms the house,
but the couple who get along well. -Madagascan

Choose your fellow traveler before you start on your journey. -Nigerois

If you are building a house and a nail breaks, do you stop building,
or do you change the nail? -Swahili

Where I make a living, there is my home. -Somalian

The person going home is not stopped by the dusk. -Bemba

The house roof fights with the rain, but he who is sheltered ignores it. -Wolof

Don't ask news of an old person, ask it of a traveler. -Oromo

When you go to the house of someone who is squatting,
don't ask for a chair. -Ghanian

93

Abroad we look at a man's clothes; at home we look at the man. -Chinese

In the ant's house the dew is a flood. -Iranian

Better than a feast elsewhere is a meal at home of tea and rice. -Japanese

A house consumes standing still, an elephant when moving. -Tamil

The lamp of one house cannot light two houses. -Chinese

Examine the neighborhood before you choose your house. -Chinese

Every dog is a great barker at the door of his own house. -Arabian

A small tumbledown house is better than a communal palace. -Arabian

It is easier to visit your friends than to live with them. -Chinese

A donkey that travels abroad will not return a horse. -Hebrew

When traveling do not calculate the distance, at dinner don't think of how much. -Chinese

No matter how much the wise man travels, he always lives in the same place. -Chinese

The wise man and the tortoise travel but never leave their home. -Chinese

If there are two cooks in one house, the soup is either too salty or too cold. -Iranian

The earth is a host who kills his guests. -Iranian

If you are traveling towards the East, you will inevitably move away from the West. -Japanese

By wisdom a house is built, and through understanding it is established; through knowledge its rooms are filled with rare and beautiful treasures. -Biblical

A large family gives beauty to a house. -Tamil

God bless him who pays visits—short visits. -Arabian

The farmer hopes for rain, the traveler for fine weather. -Chinese

That is a wise delay which makes the road safe. -English

The dog with many homes dies of hunger. -Slovakian

Make not the door wider than the house. -English

A fool knows more in his own house than a wise man in another's. -English

Better repair the gutter than the whole house. -Portuguese

If there is room in your heart there is room in your house. -Danish

The heaviest baggage for a traveler is an empty purse. -German

The fingers of the housewife do more than a yoke of oxen. -German

Empty houses are **full** of noises.
-Basque

The smoke of my own house is better than another man's fire. -Italian

A guest sees more in an hour than the host in a year. -Polish

If you are traveling in the blind man's country close one eye. -Romanian

You cannot buy wisdom abroad if there is none at home. -Russian

It is no fun to guard a house with two doors. -Spanish

Every road has two directions. -Ukrainian

However bright the sun may shine, leave not your cloak at home. -Spanish

Any road leads to the end of the world. -English

A step over the threshold is half the journey. -Welsh

The quieter you travel, the farther you'll get. -Russian

The sun at home warms better than the sun abroad. -Albanian

If three people say you are an
ass, put on a bridle. -Spanish

If the dog's prayer were ac-
cepted, there would be a
shower of bones from heaven.
-Turkish

If I die, I forgive you; if I
recover, we shall see. -Spanish

If every day was a sunny day,
who would not wish for rain?
-Japanese

If all men pulled in one
direction, the world would
topple over. -Yiddish

If the king says that it is night in
the middle of the day, look up
at the stars. -Arabian

If God were living on earth,
people would break His windows.
-Yiddish

If everyone swept in front of
his house, the whole town
would be clean. -Polish

If it must always be better, it
can never be good enough.
-Yiddish

If fools went not to market,
bad wares would not be sold.
-Spanish

However much the beetle is afraid it will
not stop the lizard swallowing it. -Fulani

Fear of the grave comes with old age. -Swahili

The smaller the lizard the greater the hope of becoming a crocodile. -African

Proportion your expenses to what you have, not what you expect. -Nigerois

It is the path you do not fear that the wild beast catches you on. -Ashanti

The half-blind person does not give up the hope of seeing again. -Oromo

Hope nourishes the living. -Fulani

Hope is the pillar of the world. -Kanuri

Don't give up hope until you fill in the grave. -Ugandan

Fire devours the grass, but not the roots. -Ewe

What one hopes for is better than what one finds. -Galla

What you yearn for makes you throw away what you have. -Ugandan

Where the heart longs to be the path never reaches. -Shona

If you are wearing shoes, you don't fear the thorns. -Sudanese

A corpse does not fear the grave. -Oromo

A fearful person would not drink water from heaven. -Oromo

A person is afraid of a forest with no leopard. -Basotho

An animal that has just escaped from a trap fears a bent stick. -Annang

The elephant does not bite, it is that trunk one fears. -Hausa

Fear surrounds the place where a snake disappeared in the bush. -Jabo

There is no hope of fruit from a tree which has been robbed
of its flowers by the frost. -Tibetan

Only death itself can end our hope. -Arabian

Even a sheep with the skin of a tiger is afraid of the wolf. -Chinese

Hope for a miracle, but don't rely on it. -Hebrew

The man who has mounted an elephant will not fear
the bark of a dog. -Indian

The firm tree does not fear the storm. -Indonesian

Fear those who do not fear God. -Iranian

A newborn baby
has no fear
of tigers. -Korean

Fear to let fall a drop, will always make you spill a lot. -Malaysian

Low is the mountain, high the expectations. -Malaysian

A remedy without pain is not to be hoped for. -Turkish

One year bitten by a snake, for three years afraid of a grass rope. -Chinese

Hope deferred makes the heart sick,
but a longing fulfilled is a tree of life. -Biblical

Do you see a man wise in his own eyes?
There is more hope for a fool than for him. -Biblical

Fear God and keep his commandments, for this is
the whole duty of man. -Biblical

When night comes, fear is at the door; when day comes,
fear is on the hills. -Pashtun

Hope is born of despair. -Iranian

Hope without work is like a tree without fruit. -Lebanese

Coffin carriers desire the year of the plague. -Japanese

Pure gold does not fear the furnace. -Chinese

Be always a little afraid so that you never have need
of being much afraid. -Finnish

Bear with evil and expect good. -English

If not for the fear of punishment, it would be sweet to sin. -Yiddish

It is folly to fear what one cannot avoid. -Danish

If you're afraid to get wet, you'll never make a good fisherman. -Armenian

A fool hopes to get honey, even from wasps. -Russian

The grave is already dug and man still continues to hope. -Yiddish

Better hazard once than be always in fear. -English

Hope is the dream of the waking. -Danish

He that lives in hope dances without music. -English

Hope is as cheap as despair. -English

Love and fear cannot be hidden. -Russian

Hope is a great breakfast but a poor dinner. -Czech

Hope for the best, but prepare for the worst. -English

If it were not for hope, the heart would break. -Greek

Short is the road that leads from fear to hatred. -Italian

Even the hardest of winters fears the spring. -Lithuanian

It is never winter in the land of hope. -Russian

Don't be afraid of a spot that can be removed with water. -Spanish

Worry often gives a small thing a big shadow. -Swedish

He who knows his heart mistrusts
his eyes. -Chinese

He who is thirsty dreams that
he is drinking. -Chinese

She who hurries cannot walk
with dignity. -Chinese

He who knows himself
knows everybody. -Chinese

He who knows does not
talk, he who talks does not
know. -Korean

She who has seen little marvels
much. -Chinese

She who has to deal with a
blockhead has need of much
brain. -Spanish

She who hears one side only,
hears nothing. -English

She who has suffered can
sympathize with those in pain.
-Bihar

He who knows himself as
well as his opponent will be
invincible. -Korean

A wife is like a blanket; when you cover yourself with it, it irritates you, and yet if you cast it aside you feel cold. -Ashanti

In a beloved wife there is no evil. -Jabo

A woman's clothes are the price her husband pays for peace. -Bantu

If you are too shy of your mother-in-law, your wife does not treat you well. -Ghanian

A husband who has a wicked wife grows old sadly. -Oromo

When a man who has many wives is sick, he dies of starvation. -Ghanian

One fights with his wife but not with his child. -Ghanian

She cried for marriage and when married she cried again. -Oromo

A bad wife is like a dirty cloth—if you travel with it, you are not clean. -Ghanian

A good wife is more precious than gold. -Ghanian

A home carries weight because of the husband. -Lugbara

A house that leaks is like a wife that nags. -Oromo

A reputation that has gone and a wife who has gone off never return. -Oromo

A vessel that the wife broke is considered as though put aside. -Oromo

A wife and a plough handle are best when shorter than the man. -Oromo

As water takes on the color of the earth so a wife takes on the manners of her husband. -Oromo

It is a man's responsibility to hunt an animal and to marry a wife. -Oromo

It is better to be content with a bad husband than to wish for the good husband of someone else. -Oromo

The cowardly husband runs away when his wife is being beaten. -Oromo

The husband of a nagging wife does not hurry home. -Oromo

When husband and wife agree with each other, they can
dry up the ocean with buckets. -Vietnamese

When a divorced man marries a divorced woman,
there are four opinions in the marriage bed. -Hebrew

A good dog does not bite a chicken and a good man
does not hit his wife. -Chinese

A girl receives, a widow takes her husband. -Chinese

If you would be happy for a week, take a wife;
if you would be happy for a month, kill a pig;
but if you would be happy all your life, plant a garden. -Chinese

A man thinks that he knows it, but his wife knows better. -Chinese

Even the thinnest piece of meat will happily marry a piece of bread.
-Turkish

To have beautiful servant girls is a threat to good marriages. -Chinese

Never strike your wife, not even with a flower. -Indian

The soldier's wife is always a widow. -Indian

The bride who wears four petticoats has a lot to hide. -Iranian

A quarrelsome wife is like a constant dripping. -Biblical

A wife of noble character who can find? She is worth
far more than rubies. -Biblical

A wife's long tongue is the staircase by which misfortunes
ascend to the house. -Chinese

A wife is a household treasure. -Japanese

Take a good wife even if you have to sell your pots and kettles. -Japanese

A wife is sought for her virtue, a concubine for her beauty. -Chinese

Curse not your wife in the evening, or you will have to sleep alone. -Chinese

It's hard to be a good wife if your husband's sisters aren't married. -Chinese

A wife should not hold conversation
with her husband's younger brother. -Chinese

A wife's advice is not worth much, but woe to the husband
who refuses to take it. -Welsh

Three corners of the house rest upon the wife;
the fourth upon the husband. -Slovakian

He's a good horse that never stumbled,
and a better wife that never grumbled. -Scottish

A wife should be as humble as a lamb, busy as a bee, as beautiful
as a bird of paradise and faithful as a turtle dove. -Russian

If the husband drinks, half the house is burning;
if the wife drinks, the whole house is ablaze. -Russian

The husband is the head, the wife is the neck;
she can turn him whichever way she wants. -Russian

It is better to marry a quiet fool than a witty scold. -English

A house needs a wife and a cat.
-Norwegian

Happy the marriage where the husband is the head
and the wife the heart. -Estonian

Marriage with peace is this world's Paradise;
with strife, this life's Purgatory. -English

Prudent men choose frugal wives. -German

Do not choose your wife at a dance,
but in the field among the harvesters. -Czech

If you want to love your household as much as your bread then you will
have to knead your wife like dough. -French

If you lose your wife and fifteen pennies—
oh ! what a pity about the money. -French

The wife cries before the wedding, the husband after. -Luxembourgian

A good wife and a wholesome cabbage soup,
what more could you want? -Russian

If your wife tells you to throw yourself off a cliff, pray to God
that it is a low one. -Spanish

The wife is the key of the house. -English

A wise woman will marry the man who loves her
rather than the one she loves. -Slovenian

The better workman, the worse husband. -English

If you have no enemies think
then that your own mother
might have produced one.
-Bulgarian

If you stay long enough in
one place the whole world
passes you by. -Chinese

If you see a strange thing and
do not regard it as strange, its
strangeness will vanish. -Chinese

If you go to bed hungry, you'll
wake up without having slept.
-Lithuanian

If you fall into a pit. Providence
is under no obligation to come
and look for you. -Iranian

If triangles had a God, He'd have
three sides. -Yiddish

If you do without something for
long enough, then you don't
need it. -Chinese

If you are going to steal bells
plug your ears. -Mongolian

If you can't hold on to the horse's
mane then don't try to hang on to
its tail. -Serbo-Croatian

If you chase after two rabbits, you
won't catch even one. -Russian

If you destroy a bridge, be sure you can swim. -Swahili

If the cockroach refuses to stay in its hole, the chicken
refuses to stay hungry. -Annang

If the elephant were not in the wilderness, buffalo would be the greatest. -Jabo

If you are not going to bite, don't show your teeth. -Ivorian

If there were no wrongdoing, there would be no forgiveness. -Egyptian

If you take your tongue to the pawnshop, you can't redeem it later. -Ghanian

If the judge is against you, you should withdraw the complaint. -Moroccan

If the panther knew how much he is feared, he would do much more harm. -Cameroonian

If crocodiles eat their own eggs
what would they do to the flesh of a frog. -Nigerian

If you put a razor in your mouth, you will spit blood. -Nigerian

If you grind damp rice, it sticks to the mortar. -Jabo

If you spend your profits before they come, then you don't have anything
to spend when you're finished trading. -Ghanian

If your son turns out to be a thief, give him up
even though he will be mad. -Moroccan

If your mother dies, you won't die; but if she is disgraced
you are also disgraced. -Ghanian

If the python knew when it was dawn, would it sleep in the daytime? -Ghanian

If you want heaven to know, tell it to the wind. -Oji

If a flint stone is lying at the bottom of a river,
the power of striking fire never passes over it. -Ghanian

If the river flows and stands in one place, it is called a pond. -Ghanian

If you go too near your relatives, they will not respect you. -Ghanian

105

If you are carrying a bag of corn that breaks open,
you don't ask the whereabouts of the Dutch ship. -Ghanian

If your fields are not plowed, your store house will be empty. -Chinese

If there is food left over in the kitchen,
there are poor people in the street. -Chinese

If fortune turns against you,
even the horse in the stable becomes a donkey. -Iranian

If you believe in gambling, in the end you will sell your house. -Chinese

If the heart is firm, the body is cool. -Chinese

If one morning you make a false step,
a hundred lifetimes cannot redeem it. -Chinese

If good luck comes, who doesn't?
If good luck does not come, who does? -Chinese

If in excess even nectar is poison. -Tamil

If man cheats the earth, the earth will cheat man. -Chinese

If a little money does not go out, great money will not come in. -Chinese

If begging should unfortunately be your lot,
knock at the large gates only. -Arabian

If you want to hit your mother-in-law, be sure to split her head. -Arabian

If you want to kill a snake, chop off its head. -Arabian

If cooks quarrel, the roast burns. -Chinese

If heaven above lets fall a plum, open your mouth. -Chinese

If one word does not succeed, ten thousand are of no avail. -Chinese

If you can't give any sugar then speak sweetly. -Indian

If you throw a handful of stones, one at least will hit. -Indian

If you are going to kill, then kill an elephant; if you
are going to steal make sure it's a treasure. -Indian

If you go into a goat stable, bleat;
if you go into a waterbuffalo stable, bellow. -Indonesian

If you don't grease the axle, you won't be able to travel. -Russian

If you can't endure the bad, you'll not live to witness the good. -Yiddish

If better were within, better would come out. -Scottish

If you are going to do something carelessly,
it would be better to give it up entirely. -Russian

If one could do charity without money and favors without aggravation,
the world would be full of saints. -Yiddish

If you can't use your eyes, follow your nose. -Latvian

If you cannot say it, point to it with your finger. -French

If you cannot **serve,**
you cannot **rule.** -Bulgarian

If every lie were to knock out a tooth, many would be toothless. -Swedish

If lies are to find credence, they must be patched with truth. -Danish

If luck plays along, cleverness succeeds. -Yiddish

If a man knew where he would fall he would spread straw first. -Russian

If a man once falls, all will tread on him. -English

If the wise men play the fool, they do it with a vengeance. -English

If your neighbor is an early riser, you too will become one. -Albanian

If you shoot your arrows at stones, you will damage them. -Austrian

If you want apples, you have to shake the trees. -Bulgarian

If you call one wolf, you invite the pack. -Bulgarian

If the fire does not burn you the smoke will blacken you. -French

If you live in Rome, don't quarrel with the Pope. -French

He who is his own teacher has a
fool for his pupil.
-German

He who is sure of his victory will
not start a war. -Chinese

She who is dependent on others
must make friends with the dog.
-Japanese

He who is pierced with
thorns must limp off to him
who has a lancet. -Yoruba

He who is kind to the poor lends to
the LORD, and he will reward him
for what he has done. -Biblical

She who is a friend of the forest cannot be an enemy of the
tree. -Russian

She who is afraid of doing too
much always does too little.
-German

She who is always right will
never get round the world.
-Japanese

She who is a guest in two
houses, starves. -Indian

He who is looking for a place
to sleep doesn't tell you that
he wets the bed. -Ghanian

If you are young, do not laugh at a short person. -Ghanian

If you are poor and you grow old, it isn't noticed. -Ghanian

If the turtle wants to trouble his wife, he tells her to plait the hair
falling down his back (and let him be off in search of some fun). -Ghanian

If the pot doesn't break, the pit where the clay is dug
will never become wide. -Ghanian

If those who are coming to kill you today say they will kill you tomorrow,
let them kill you today and then you can rest immediately. -Ghanian

If you are a good listener and you advise someone, he listens. -Ghanian

If you applaud with one hand
it will not be heard. -Ovambo

If you get mixed with bran you'll soon be pecked by chickens. -Libyan

If you demand payment of your mother's debt,
the payment falls on your father. -Ghanian

If your eyes are higher than your eyebrows, you get lost. -Ghanian

If a man preserves something, he puts it
where he can find it when he wants it. -Ghanian

If you keep throwing your things away,
you'll find them when you are poor. -Ghanian

If the bush dog were rich, he would not have gone along
the river banks digging for crabs. -Ghanian

If even the antelope who rules the state is resting peacefully, why should
the leopard take up arms to go to war in defense of the state? -Ghanian

If you hold back an old woman, don't fight for the palm wine she has. -Ghanian

If there was any value in drinking, the beetle would not
breathe through his back. -Ghanian

If you do not gather firewood you cannot keep warm. -Ovambo

If everyone thought alike, no goods would be sold. -Libyan

If the bird drinks not at the stream, it knows its own watering place. -Wolof

109

If you haven't been to two marketplaces,
you don't know which is the best value. -Fulani

If you can give me no ointment for my wound, can you help me
by not rubbing salt in? -Iranian

If you are going out for a fight leave your best hat at home. -Japanese

If one man praises you, a thousand will repeat the praise. -Japanese

If you are going to sit on it for three years,
the seat will certainly get warm. -Japanese

If you think about things too long, good thoughts will disappear. -Japanese

If you cannot build a town, build a heart. -Kurdish

If you fall in love let her be a beauty; if you should steal,
let it be a camel. -Lebanese

"If" married "But" and their child was called "Maybe." -Iranian

If you follow the lead of the cockerel, you'll be led to the poulterer. -Lebanese

If you are going to bathe, get thoroughly wet. -Malaysian

If you dip your arm into the pickle pot let it be up to the elbow. -Malaysian

If you are sick, think about your life; if you are better,
think about your gold. -Mongolian

If your beard's on fire, others will light their pipes on it. -Turkish

If you give people nuts, you'll get shells thrown at you. -Yemeni

If you know where to stop and stop there,
you will never be disgraced. -Chinese

If the time has passed, there is no point in preparing. -Yemeni

If a thorn sticks into the flesh,
a sharp thorn must be used to draw it out. -Thai

If not today—when? -Indian

If a man's heart be impure, all things will appear hostile to him. -Sanskrit

If you hate a man, let him live. -Japanese

If the moon helps me I will scoff at the stars. -Georgian

If you want equality, then go to the graveyard. -German

If you heat an empty pot it bursts. -German

If you let the weeds grow for a year you will need
seven to clear them. -German

If you cannot catch a fish, do not blame the sea. -Greek

If it's not burning you why cool it? -Dutch

If you would succeed, you must not be too good. -Italian

If you don't crack the shell, you can't eat the nut. -Russian

If you want to marry wisely, **marry your equal.** -Spanish

If you would be pope, you must think of nothing else. -Spanish

If you want good service, serve yourself. -Spanish

If the sky falls there will be pots broken. -Spanish

If you take care of the soil, the soil will take care of you. -Latvian

If you keep on talking, you will end up saying
what you didn't intend to say. -Yiddish

If you tickle yourself you can laugh when you like. -Russian

If you haven't given your word, restrain yourself;
if you have, keep it. -Russian

If God drenches you with His rain, He will dry you with His sun. -Slovenian

If you would live long, open your heart. -Bulgarian

If a fool holds the cow by the horns, a clever man can milk her. -Yiddish

If God wants people to suffer,
he sends them too much understanding. -Yiddish

It is good to know the truth and to speak the truth. It Is even better to know the truth and speak about palm trees. -Arabian

It is no time to play chess when the house is on fire. -Italian

Indecision is like the stepchild: if he doesn't wash his hands, he is called dirty; if he does, he is wasting the water. -Madagascan

It is not easy to sting a bear with a straw. -Danish

It is difficult to throw a stone at a lizard clinging to an earthen water pot. -Ghanian

Intelligence consists in recognizing opportunity. -Chinese

It is better to build bridges than walls. -Swahili

In the village that you don't know, the chickens have teeth. -Ivorian

It is easy to throw anything into the river, but difficult to take it out again. -Kashmiri

It is because of shyness that father Ananse wears an antelope's skin hat when he goes to ask people to help him in weeding his farm. -Ghanian

If you are in hiding, don't light a fire. -Ghanian

If you try to cleanse others—
just like soap, you will waste away in the process! -Madagascan

If the hill is on fire the grasshoppers are roasted. -Madagascan

If a rich man steals it is a mistake;
if a poor man makes a mistake he has stolen. -Moroccan

If you have run out of gunpowder, use your gun as a club. -Nigerian

If you had teeth of steel, you could eat iron coconuts. -Wolof

If you climb up a tree, you must climb down the same tree. -Sierra Leonean

If the full moon loves you, why worry about the stars? -Tunisian

If the vulture gives advice to the hyena, **he takes it.**
-Ghanian

If you do not rise when you do not want to,
you will not arrive when you want to. -Fulani

If you do not have thoughts you do not have understanding. -Ovambo

If the paddle says it knows the bottom of the river, it
doesn't know it as well as the fish hook. -Ghanian

If a rope is long it gets entangled. -Ghanian

If you are merciful to the antelope, you go to bed hungry. -Ghanian

If you give yourself away here and there,
you find a ready helper when in need. -Ghanian

If a drunkard throws a punch, he falls down. -Ghanian

If all seeds that fall were to grow,
then no one could follow the path under the trees. -Nigerian

If a hunter kills a buffalo in the bush, he must bring back a tail. -Swahili

If the natives eat rats, eat rats. -Swahili

If they are offered winged ants, people will eat them. -African

IF & THEN -3

113

If Heaven creates a man, there must be some use for him. -Chinese

If you don't drink, the price of wine is of no interest. -Chinese

If the bird had not sung, it wouldn't have been shot. -Japanese

If the end is good everything is good. -Japanese

If you have happiness, don't use it all up. -Chinese

If the heart be stout, a mouse can lift an elephant. -Tibetan

If you continually grind a bar of iron, you can make a needle of it. -Chinese

If there is a lid that does not fit there is a lid that does. -Japanese

If you suspect a man, don't employ him;
if you employ a man, don't suspect him. -Chinese

If you bow at all, bow low. -Chinese

If you don't climb the high mountain, you can't view the plain. -Chinese

If you don't know where you are going,
look back to where you've come from. -Arabian

If you must play, decide upon three things at the start:
the rules of the game, the stakes, and when to stop. -Chinese

If an eel is with fish, he shows his tail; if he is with snakes,
he shows his head. -Indonesian

If you hear that a mountain has moved, believe; but if you hear that a man
has changed his character, believe it not. -Islamic

If you are going into the wood—don't leave your axe at home. -Thai

"If and "when" were planted, and "nothing" grew. -Turkish

If you want to gather a lot of knowledge, act as if you are ignorant.
-Vietnamese

If you are standing upright, don't worry if your shadow is crooked. -Chinese

If you are up to your knees in pleasure,
then you are up to your waist in grief. -Indian

If you have no arrows in your quiver, go not with archers. -German

If you lie down with the dogs, you get up with the fleas. -Yiddish

If you cross over the fence, you acquire other ideas. -Yiddish

If you invest in a fever, you will realize a disease. -Yiddish

If you want to lose your friend, grant him a loan. -Estonian

If you would have the lamp burn, you must pour oil into it. -German

If not for the light, there would be no shadow. -Yiddish

If you will stir up the mire, you must bear the smell. -Danish

If your heart is a **rose**, then your mouth will speak **perfumed** words.
-Russian

If you talk to an official you must talk rubles. -Russian

If you are a fast talker at least think slowly. -Cretan

If your head is made of butter, don't be a baker. -Danish

If the sea water were hotter we could catch boiled fish. -French

If you have a good cellar at home don't go drinking at the tavern. -Italian

If you live with wolves learn to howl. -Spanish

If envy would burn, there would be no use for wood. -Yugoslavian

If things were to be done twice, all would be wise. -English

If the fool knew how to be silent he could sit among the wise. -Czech

If you've enjoyed the dance, pay the musicians. -German

If it is good then the deed is more important than the intention;
if it's bad then the intention is worse than the deed. -Spanish

He who is full loathes honey, but
to the hungry even what is bitter
tastes sweet. -Biblical

He who is covered with
other people's clothes is
naked. -Tunisian

She who is desperate will
squeeze oil out of a grain
of sand. -Japanese

He who is cutting a path
doesn't see that it is crooked
behind him. -Ghanian

He who is everybody's
friend is either very poor or
very rich. -Spanish

She who is guilty is the one who
has much to say. -Ashanti

She who is struck by the light-
ning doesn't hear the thunder.
-Hungarian

She who is in a hurry always
arrives late. -Georgian

She who is guilty has much
to say. -Ghanian

He who is drunk from wine
can sober up, he who is
drunk from wealth cannot.
-African

When a baby grows, the crying changes. -Annang

A girl laughs after she has finished housework. -Shona

When the mouse laughs at the cat, there is a hole. -Wolof

Sadness is a valuable treasure—only discovered in people you love. -Madagascan

Reading books removes sorrows from the heart. -Moroccan

"Oh river water what makes you cry?" "The stones against my current!"
"Oh stones what makes you cry?" "The running water!" -Oromo

The creeper with large thorns does something to make us laugh
and it also does something to make us cry. -Ghanian

When someone is crying, your crying helps him. -Ghanian

Even where death has occurred people still laugh. -Basotho

A matter which is in one place causes laughter,
at another place causes tears. -Ghanian

There is no joy in forced laughter. -Lugbara

What makes some people laugh, makes other people cry. -Ghanian

Laughing she got pregnant; crying she delivered. -Oromo

The person who is always laughing
appears to be laughing when he is dying. -Oromo

The place where you are happy is better than the place you were born. -Ghanian

Birth is the remedy for sorrow. -Hausa

The efforts of the poor are their tears. -Egyptian

It's the mother who can cure her child's tears. -Hausa

A child who does not cry suffers even while being carried on the back
of her mother. -Basotho

While the cattle moo and cry for their dead,
the donkey keeps on grazing. -Oromo

117

Earth laughs at him who calls a place his own. -Hindustani

Joy and grief must be regulated by moderation. -Tamil

It is one life whether we spend it in laughing or weeping. -Japanese

He hit me, started to cry, and went straight to the judge to sue me. -Arabian

A small cottage wherein laughter lives is worth more than a castle full of tears. -Chinese

If you have nothing else to offer me, offer me your smile. -Chinese

You will never be punished for making people die of laughter. -Chinese

What soap is for the body, tears are for the soul. -Hebrew

Be careful not to make a woman weep. God counts her tears. -Hebrew

One Joy scatters a hundred griefs. -Chinese

A man laughs at others and weeps for himself. -Indian

Smiles that you broadcast, will always come back to you. -Indian

Every tear has a smile behind it. -Iranian

The dog called "Sorrow," without eating, will be fat in every house. -Japanese

Time spent laughing is time spent with the gods. -Japanese

Our pleasures are shallow; our sorrows are deep. -Chinese

Each heart knows its own bitterness, and no one else can share its joy. -Biblical

Even in laughter the heart may ache, and joy may end in grief. -Biblical

It takes great wisdom to laugh at one's own misfortunes. -Hindi

The desire to laugh is stronger than the desire to weep. -Burmese

Neither with curses nor with laughter can you change the world. -Yiddish

Every day brings forth its own sorrows. -Yiddish

The end of mirth is the beginning of sorrow. -Dutch

Joy and sorrow are next-door neighbors. -German

The drunken man's joy is often the sober man's sorrow. -Danish

Laughter is heard farther than weeping. -Yiddish

Learn weeping and you shall laugh gaining. -English

What a wise man bewails makes the fool happy. -Yiddish

A tear in the eye is the wound of the heart. -Gypsy

Joy and sorrow sleep in the same bed.
-Czech

The person who loves sorrow will always find something
to moan about. -Danish

Those who tickle themselves may laugh when they please. -German

He wastes his tears who weeps before the judge. -Italian

Sweet are the tears that are dried by your loved one. -Portuguese

When sorrow is asleep, wake it not. -Romanian

When you live next to the cemetery you cannot weep for everyone. -Russian

Shared joy is a double joy; shared sorrow is half a sorrow. -Swedish

One does not live on joy or die of sorrow. -Yiddish

Sadness and gladness succeed each other. -English

Sin enters laughing and comes out crying. -Romanian

If you wait long enough, it will be
good weather. -Japanese

In his dreams a mouse
can frighten a cat.
-Armenian

In a place without dogs
they teach the cats
to bark. -Georgian

In a deserted village the
jackass is king. -Indian

If you touch a hot coal you
burn yourself; a cold one,
you blacken yourself. -Greek

In a tree that you can't climb,
there are always a
thousand fruits. -Indian

In a fight the rich man tries
to save his face, the poor man
his coat. -Russian

If you want your dreams to
come true, don't sleep. -Yiddish

If you wake up in the morning
and feel no pain it is to be feared
that you died in the night. -Czech

If you want to drown yourself,
don't torture yourself with
shallow water. -Bulgarian

If one could know where death resided, one would never stop there. -Ashanti

A fly does not mind dying in coconut cream. -Swahili

If a dead tree falls, it carries with it a live one. -Kenyan

Life is a shadow and a mist; it passes quickly by, and is no more. -Madagascan

The dying person cannot wait for the shroud to be woven. -Madagascan

Living is not a reward and dying is no crime. -Madagascan

Birth is the only remedy against death. -Nigerois

All people will die, but we want a good death. -Ghanian

Death has no modesty.
-Zulu

If you are looking for a good place to live, the place
where you already live is good. -Ghanian

Man is always walking near his own grave. -Ghanian

The day it wishes death, the goat licks the nose of the leopard. -Oromo

Life is difficult. -Ghanian

Nobody takes a dead person's amulet and says to it:
"Give me life and health!" -Ghanian

The hoe of death does not weed in only one place. -Ghanian

What is said over the dead lion's body, could not be said to him alive. -Congolese

Every kind of death is the same. -Ghanian

Death does not exclude anyone. -Lugbara

The teeth of death are sharp. -Lugbara

Once one is born, one's death is inevitable. -Oromo

Wise birds live in carefully chosen trees. -Japanese

A living body is a dying body. -Japanese

The distant grove you see surrounds either a house or a grave. -Chinese

For each man to whom Heaven gives birth,
the earth provides a grave. -Chinese

Life is like the flame of a lamp; it needs a little oil now and again. -Kashmiri

Death rides a fast camel. -Arabian

To be able to curse once a day improves happiness
and lengthens life. -Chinese

To die is to stop living but to stop living is something
entirely different than dying. -Chinese

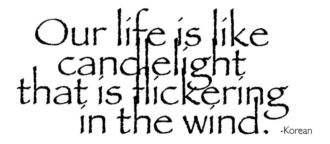

Our life is like candlelight that is flickering in the wind. -Korean

The earth offers you a grave everywhere. -Chinese

Death is the bride of life. -Indonesian

He is still alive because he cannot afford a funeral. -Iranian

It is easy to die—the difficulty lies in living. -Japanese

The living are denied a table; the dead get a whole coffin. -Mongolian

Above all else, guard your heart, for it is the wellspring of life. -Biblical

Like the fool, the wise man too must die! -Biblical

The dust returns to the ground it came from, and the spirit
returns to God who gave it. -Biblical

Life is like perpetual drunkenness, the pleasure passes
but the headache remains. -Iranian

The brave person regards dying as going home. -Chinese

Life is a long journey with a heavy bag on its back. -Japanese

We are born crying, live complaining, and die disappointed. -English

No calendar is needed for dying. -Yiddish

Death answers before it is asked. -Russian

Death is the last doctor. -Swedish

Life is no more than a dream, but don't wake me up! -Yiddish

Death squares all accounts. -English

When death is there, dying is over. -Russian

Life is half spent before we know what it is. -English

A man should stay alive **if only out of curiosity.** -Yiddish

The fall of a leaf is a whisper to the living. -Danish

Life is an onion that you peel crying. -French

Man's life is like an egg in the hands of a child. -Romanian

Death does not take the old but the ripe. -Russian

The dead open the eyes of the living. -Spanish

Life is a gift for which we pay dearly. -Spanish

Never praise life in front of death, nor the beautiful day in front of night. -Spanish

Death is God's broom. -Swedish

Life is the biggest bargain—we get it for nothing. -Yiddish

There is a remedy for all things but death. -English

He that has time has life. -English

He who installs a king
never rules with him. -Zulu

He who hides his faults
plans to make more.
-Chinese

She who laughs much,
weeps much. -Turkish

She who knows the road can
ride full trot. -Italian

He who is a slave of truth
is a free man. -Arabian

He who is born a mule
can never be a horse. -Corsican

She who is without work
in summer is without boots
in winter. -Polish

She who knows little quickly
tells it. -Italian

She who is the last to be
put in the sack is the first
to get out of it. -Latvian

He who is afraid of death,
loses his life. -Romanian

Cat and mouse cannot be neighbors long. -Ovambo

There is bound to be a knot in a very long string. -Ghanian

The one being carried does not realize how far away the town is. -Nigerian

If pleasant it will be short-lived, if unpleasant long-lived. -Fulani

Don't think of the shortness of the day, but of the length of the year. -Madagascan

When a way is long you shorten it with your feet, not with a hatchet. -Oji

No one cuts a walking stick longer than himself. -Ghanian

Truthful speech is short and a LIE is long. -Oromo

The chief's hands are long. -Basotho

If a bird remains too long in a tree, someone hits it with a stone. -Ghanian

If you are in a short line, you don't stop and go in a long one. -Ghanian

We welcome someone returning from a long journey, and not from a short journey. -Ghanian

Tall and short teeth all eat the same way. -Ghanian

When water remains too long in a bottle, it stinks. -Ghanian

Even though the antelope's tail is short, nevertheless it drives the flies away with it. -Ghanian

Speech and the stick for the donkey are better when short. -Oromo

Though it lasts for a long time, honey does not become sour. -Oromo

When evening has fallen, the dawn is far away. -Oromo

When your arm is too short lengthen it with a stick. -Nkundu-Mongo

A whole village hunting group takes long to unite. -Basotho

125

A whitewashed crow will not remain white long. -Chinese

No matter how long one may live, the day of death will come. -Tamil

Nights of pleasure are short. -Lebanese

God gave the giraffe a long neck so that He would not have to bend the palm tree. -Arabian

Borrowed money shortens time; working for others lengthens it. -Chinese

It's better to die two years early than to live one year too long. -Chinese

The flowers in your garden don't smell as sweet as those in the wild, but they last much longer. -Chinese

A day of grief lasts longer than a month of joy. -Chinese

Hold short services for minor gods. -Nepali

Long or short, a stick is always a stick; tall or short, people are always people. -Chinese

Even when months and days are long, life is short. -Japanese

The inarticulate speak longest. -Japanese

The highway is always shorter than the unknown side roads. -Turkish

Beautiful women are short lived. -Korean

If the string is long, the kite flies high. -Chinese

He that has long legs will go far. -Arabian

The rope of a lie is short. -Arabian

It's not that the well is too deep, but rather the rope is too short. -Chinese

Happy hours are very short. -Vietnamese

If one month is long, another month is shorter. -Korean

Good company on the road is the shortest of short cuts. -Italian

A day is long, but a lifetime is short. -Russian

The day is short and the work is long. -English

He that sups with the devil needs a long spoon. -English

A borrowed horse and your own spurs make short miles. -Danish

Long is not forever. -German

If you take too long to choose, you will end up
with the leftovers. -Serbo-Croatian

There are simple remedies for sausages that are too long. -Danish

The nearer the inn, the longer the road. -German

What is long spoken of happens at last. -Dutch

The tall one wouldn't bend; the short one wouldn't stretch
and the kiss was lost. -Georgian

Most people like short prayers and long sausages. -German

Let your prayers for a good crop be short and your hoeing long. -Albanian

On a long journey, even a straw weighs heavy. -Spanish

Short pleasure, long lament. -English

The road to misfortune is short. -Russian

He that runs fast will not run long. -English

Things are not as quickly achieved as conceived. -Yiddish

The thread must be longer than the needle. -Basque

The wise man has long ears and a short tongue. -German

Life is a dung pie from
which you take a bite
every day. The art is to eat
it with taste. -French

Life's caravan never turns back.
-Swahili

Look and keep silent, and if
you are eating meat, tell the
world it's fish. -Arabian

It takes a good many mice
to kill a cat. -Danish

Let anyone who despises the
position of the moon get up
and correct it. -Hausa

Knowledge is like a garden: if it
is not cultivated, it cannot be
harvested. -Guinean

Let it be worse, as long as it's
a change. -Yiddish

It is not the day on which
the yam is planted that we
fix sticks for its climbers.
-Ghanian

Just because he harmed your
goat, do not go out and kill
his bull. -Kenyan

It's good to behold
beauty and to live with
wisdom. -Yiddish

The earth is a giant cooking pot and men are the meat therein. -Madagascan

If you buy a woman, buy her for a high price, for there is
a village in her stomach. -Ghanian

The beauty of the man is in his intelligence,
and the intelligence of the woman is in her beauty. -Moroccan

Nobody knows the secrets that exist between a husband and a wife. -Ghanian

Man cries for a reason; if you see something
worth crying about, you cry. -Ghanian

What a tall woman has hung up, a short man cannot undo. -Bantu

If the men are not killed, you can't take their women. -Ghanian

The quarrel among men is solved by the vulture.
-Basotho

Rather an entertaining ugly woman than a boring beauty. -Moroccan

When a tall woman carries palm nuts, the hornbill eats them. -Ghanian

Two male animals don't live in the same den. -Ghanian

If you are patient, you can marry one of the chief's female slaves. -Ghanian

A man dies in the open, a woman indoors. -Lugbara

One does not place a bow in the hands of a woman. -Lugbara

The spoon of a woman does not know the pot of another woman. -Lugbara

A woman sulks toward the innermost part of a house. -Basotho

One who is looking for a wife
doesn't speak contemptuously of women. -Ghanian

All men want to become chiefs, and if they don't becomes chiefs
then they say chieftancy is a burden. -Ghanian

As long as there are eyes, women will put on make-up. -Oromo

Where women abound, noise abounds. -Oromo

129

Deep down all men are alike—and that is the problem. -Chinese

It's not the beauty of a woman that blinds the man,
the man blinds himself. -Chinese

When a man is crazy about a woman only she can cure him. -Chinese

The spouse of a woman is a man, the spouse of a man is his livelihood. -Indian

Who cares if a crow is male or female? -Japanese

The man is a river, the woman a lake. -Kurdish

A woman is a fortress, a man her prisoner. -Kurdish

Men and women sleep on the same pillow,
but they have different dreams. -Mongolian

Even the one-eyed man winks to women. -Arabian

Men are mountains and women are levers which move them. -Pashtun

Women look for talent, men for beauty. -Vietnamese

If a man runs after a woman, he falls into marriage;
if a woman runs after a man she falls into ruin. -Khionghta

The female heart is as unstable as water rolling on a lotus leaf. -Thai

Women's intrigues surpass those of men. -Lebanese

If someone says "There is a wedding ceremony in the clouds,"
then the women would soon arrive with their ladders. -Arabian

Don't let women who attract attention walk behind you. -Cambodian

Of all the female qualities a warm heart is the most valuable. -Chinese

Men and women are never placed too far apart to be near. -Japanese

Pears and women are the sweetest in the parts that are heaviest. -Japanese

Because of their figure, vain women stay cold. -Japanese

It is easier to bear a child once a year than to shave every day. -Russian

Woman's instinct is often truer than man's reasoning. -English

Love enters man through his eyes; woman through her ears. -Polish

The man loves with his head, the woman thinks with her heart. -Danish

To have a woman is bad; to lose her is worse. -Danish

If you want to understand men, study women. -French

Marriage teaches you to live alone. -French

Every woman needs two men—one to be married to and the other to compare. -French

A woman's heart sees more than ten men's eyes. -Swedish

Men are as old as they feel, women as old as they look. -Italian

A man's eyes are for seeing, a woman's for being seen. -Luxembourgian

Men have thought about their marriage a whole year long— and it lasts but one night. -Moorish

A ship and a woman are ever repairing. -Welsh

A woman's tongue is the last thing about her that dies. -English

By day they're ready to divorce, by night they're ready for bed. -Yiddish

Beware of women with beards and men without beards. -Basque

It is easier to make a hundred watches agree than ten women. -Polish

It is difficult to trust women. -Irish

Discreet women have neither eyes nor ears. -English

Women can keep only those secrets of which they know nothing. -Serbo-Croatian

He who hates, hates himself. -Zulu

He who has only one
enemy, meets him every-
where. -Iranian

She who lives in the attic knows
where the roof leaks. -Nigerian

He who has two women
loses his soul; he who has
two houses loses his mind.
-French

He who has studied himself is
his own master. -Tamil

She who learns, teaches.
-Ethiopian

She who lies on the ground
must expect to be trodden on.
-German

She who listens to a propo-
sition is already half sold.
-German

She who led me in the
night, will be thanked by
me at daybreak. -Bantu

He who has traveled alone can
tell what he likes. -Swahili

HE WHO ❖ SHE WHO

A child does not deride the ugliness of his mother. -Lugbara

A child is like a precious stone, but also a heavy burden. -Swahili

A child is like an axe; even if it hurts you, you still carry it on your shoulder. -Bemba

When you take a knife away from a child, give him a piece of wood instead. -Kenyan

Small children grow up. -Ghanian

When you show the moon to a child, it sees only your finger. -Bemba

Don't tell any more fairy tales when the child has gone to sleep. -Burundi

More precious than our children are the children of our children. -Egyptian

The child hates the one who gives him all he wants.
-African

For children the brave one is their father alone. -Oromo

The child who has never had indigestion eats and eats. -Bemba

By crawling, a child learns to stand. -Nigerois

Let the parent punish the child. -Swahili

A child does not break a land tortoise, but a child knows how to break a snail. -Ga

If a child always likes to be with the elders, he will grow up too fast. -Ghanian

What the family talks about in the evening the children will talk about in the morning. -Oromo

When a grown-up says something but doesn't do it, the children no longer fear him. -Ghanian

One can't give a grasshopper to a child if one has not caught it yet. -Madagascan

When the child plays in the mud-puddle he is seeking work— for his parents. -Nkundu-Mongo

A tree that is spoiled does not flower; a son that is spoiled does not benefit his parents. -Oromo

The adult looks to deeds, the child to love. -Hindustani

A child is a child though he may be the ruler of a town. -Lebanese

A deformed child is the dearer to his parents. -Japanese

Even without parents a child will grow up. -Japanese

Children do not have as much affection for parents
as parents have for them. -Japanese

Do not pray for gold and jade and precious things,
but pray that your children and grandchildren may all be good. -Chinese

Food and clothing from one's parents, knowledge from
one's teacher. -Japanese

A house without children is a graveyard. -Indian

As is the mother such is the child, as is the yarn such is the cloth. -Tamil

If you want your children to enjoy a quiet life let them suffer
a little hunger and a little cold. -Chinese

Do not confine your children to your own learning,
for they were born In another time. -Hebrew

The crab instructs its young: "Walk straight ahead—like me." -Indian

A child is a bridge to heaven. -Iranian

To understand your parents' love you must raise children yourself. -Chinese

Even between parents and children money matters make strangers. -Japanese

The child who died too soon was always beautiful and intelligent. -Japanese

Do not despise your mother when she is old. -Biblical

Worries about children continue until death. -Lebanese

Duty to parents is higher than the mountains, deeper than the sea. -Japanese

Veneration and respect must be paid to the mother
as well as to the father. -Japanese

A child is a certain worry and an uncertain joy. -Swedish

The child who gets a stepmother also gets a stepfather. -Danish

The dearer the child, the sharper must be the rod. -Danish

Children are the riches of the poor. -Danish

From bad matches good children are also born. -Yiddish

Love your children with your heart, but train them with your hands. -Russian

Who has no children does not know what love is. -Italian

Small children give you **headache;** big children, **heartache.**
-Russian

Clever father, clever daughter; clever mother, clever son. -Russian

Happy is he that is happy in his children. -English

The mother of a hero is the first to weep. -Serbo-Croatian

Our parents taught us to speak and the world taught us to be silent. -Czech

He that hath no children doth bring them up well. -English

I can chew for you, my child, but you must swallow by yourself. -Hungarian

Beloved children have many names. -Hungarian

Parents can provide everything except good luck. -Yiddish

A child with seven nannies often has an eye missing. -Russian

Children are what they are made. -French

Children have wide ears and long tongues. -English

Dividends from children are more precious than from money. -Yiddish

135

Memory does not forget the promised kiss, but the remembrance of the kiss received is soon lost. -Finnish

Nobody can prepare for the harmattan by drinking plenty of water. -Ghanian

No one puts his finger in another man's mouth and then beats him over the head. -Ashanti

Milk the cow, but don't pull off the udder. -Dutch

No one can be caught in places he does not visit. -Danish

Men are a bundle of groundnuts, only when one opens them does one know the spotted ones. -Hausa

Never tickle the nose of a sleeping bear. -German

No one knows what the elephant ate to make it so big. -Ghanian

Mud houses don't burn. -Nigerois

My donkey is dead; let no more grass grow. -Greek

Only by waiting is character known. -Hausa

The patient man cooks a stone till he drinks broth from it. -Hausa

If love is a sickness, patience is the remedy. -Cameroonian

If one is not in a hurry, even an egg will start walking. -Ethiopian

There is no queue at the gate of Patience. -Moroccan

Hurrying and worrying are not the same as strength. -Nigerois

If you do not have patience you cannot make beer. -Ovambo

The remedy against bad times is to have patience with them. -Egyptian

Begin with patience, end with pleasure. -Swahili

Where the runner goes the walker will go with patience. -Hausa

Too much speed breeds delay. -Shona

The hungry person waited until the food was cooked,
but couldn't wait until it cooled. -Oromo

By slowly collecting the container is filled. -Oromo

If you clean your teeth with a chewing stick in a hurry,
they will bleed. -Ghanian

The herbs to be applied to a snake bite are plucked quickly. -Ghanian

Because she has never given birth she is in a hurry to give birth. -Oromo

God does not hurry.
But what he sends to the earth does not fail to arrive. -Oromo

The weaver is in a hurry, but he must be patient
because the weak threads break easily. -Oromo

A bundle of elephant flesh can't be roasted in a hurry. -Nkundu-Mongo

Make haste before the road gets slippery. -Bemba

137

Men in a hurry from dawn until sunset do not live long. -Chinese

Money grows on the tree of patience. -Japanese

A fool in a hurry drinks tea with a fork. -Chinese

A moment of patience can prevent a great disaster and a moment of impatience can ruin a whole life. -Chinese

Have patience, the grass will be milk soon enough. -Chinese

A patient woman can roast an ox with a lantern. -Chinese

Patience is the most beautiful prayer. -Indian

Work is twice done by the man in a hurry. -Iranian

Patience, and the mulberry leaf becomes a silk gown.
-Chinese

A proposal without patience breaks its own heart. -Japanese

Patience is the key to paradise. -Turkish

Patience is bitter but its fruit is sweet. -Japanese

Patience will pierce even a rock. -Japanese

The end of haste is repentance. -Turkish

Better a patient man than a warrior, a man who controls his temper than one who takes a city. -Biblical

Two things cannot be done at one time. -Japanese

In haste there is error. -Chinese

Patience is safety, haste is blame. -Turkish

Hurry men at their work, not at their meals. -Chinese

When you are in a hurry, the horse holds back. -Chinese

The only cure for sorrow is to kill it with patience. -Irish

If you have the desire, you must also have patience. -Russian

If you drive slowly, you'll arrive more quickly. -Yiddish

The fish comes to the rod of him who waits. -Estonian

He that is too much in haste may stumble on a good road. -French

All is not lost that is delayed. -French

Do not be in a hurry to tie what you cannot untie. -English

There is no science without patience. -French

God did not create haste. -Finnish

Patience is often better than medicine. -German

The future is for those who know how to wait. -Russian

For what cannot be cured, patience is the best remedy. -Irish

Patience and hard work will overcome everything. -Russian

One who is waiting thinks the time long. -Irish

There is not a tree in heaven higher than the tree of patience. -Irish

After taking ninety-nine years to climb a stairway, the tortoise falls and says there is a curse on haste. -Maltese

However early you get up you cannot hasten the dawn. -Spanish

Nothing should be done in a hurry except catching fleas. -German

The greater the haste, the greater the hindrance. -Welsh

Who hastens to live soon dies. -Russian

139

He who has no falcon
must hunt with an owl.
-Danish

He who has nothing depends on
him who has something. -Ghanian

She who loves honey should be
patient of the stinging of the bees.
-Moroccan

He who has not married nor
built a house doesn't know
where his money has gone.
-Libyan

He who has no shoes dances
in his socks. -German

She who lives on hope dies
of hunger. -Turkish

She who looks for light work
goes very tired to bed. -Yiddish

She who loves a thing often
talks of it. -Egyptian

She who looks for a friend
without a fault will never
find one. -Armenian

He who has no spoon will
burn his hands. -Mauritanian

If stretching were wealth, the cat would be rich. -Ga

A child does not know his father's poverty. -Kpelle

A poor man cannot afford to have whims. -Swahili

The poor man and the rich man do not play together. -Ashanti

If you get rich, be in a dark corner when you jump for joy. -African

The monkey says there is nothing better than poverty
to unlearn man of his conceit. -Ghanian

When you are rich, you are resented; when you are poor,
you are despised. -Ghanian

The rich man never dances badly. -Swahili

Work is the medicine for poverty. -Yoruba

Wealth diminishes with usage; learning increases with use. -Zanzibari

If youthful pride were wealth, then every man
would have had it in his lifetime. -Ghanian

When your riches are getting exhausted, you come to your senses. -Ghanian

If you get rich, share some of your wealth with others. -Ghanian

"Get rich, die quickly!" is not said. -Ghanian

If the poor man wears gold, people say it is brass. -Ghanian

Only the poor person knows God. -Oromo

The coming of poverty upon a person is imperceivable. -Oromo

Poverty is like a hornless cow. -Basotho

When a rich man is drunk, people say he is sick. -Ghanian

When a rich person dies, there is astonishment;
when a poor person dies, nobody notices. -Oromo

Dogs show no aversion to poor families. -Chinese

Without illness and diseases one can get rich very soon. -Vietnamese

The poor can only guess at what wealth is;
the rich don't know what poverty means. -Chinese

Poverty and ugliness are difficult to hide. -Chinese

The only thing that was missing at the rich man's funeral
was mourners. -Chinese

Poverty runs after the poor, wealth after the rich. -Hebrew

The poor looks for food and the rich man for appetite. -Indian

There is a great uproar made about the debt of a poor man. -Indian

Wealth without learning is like beauty without chastity. -Tamil

The voice of the poor has no echo. -Indian

Poverty destroys all virtues. -Indian

Poverty makes thieves, like love makes poets. -Indian

There are three uncertainties: woman, wind, and wealth. -Indian

A rich man can't afford revolutions. -Iranian

If a rich man eats a snake people say, "This is wisdom!"
If a poor man eats a snake people say, "This is folly!" -Lebanese

The rich eat kebab, the poor inhale smoke. -Tajik

When a rich man falls they say it was an accident;
when a poor man falls they say that he was drunk. -Turkish

The rich become deaf and the mighty blind. -Vietnamese

Wealth brings many friends, but a poor man's friend deserts him. -Biblical

Give me neither poverty nor riches. -Biblical

Old age and poverty are wounds that can't be healed. -Greek

Contentment is the greatest wealth. -English

Debt is the worst poverty. -English

When God wants to make a poor man happy, he makes him lose his donkey and then find it again. -Armenian

Knowledge makes one laugh, but wealth makes one dance. -English

Better poor on land than rich at sea. -Dutch

All riches come from the earth. -Armenian

The poor are cured by work, the rich by the doctor. -Polish

When you are rich you suffer in a more comfortable way. -French

If a bird knew how poor he was it wouldn't sing so beautifully. -Danish

Misfortune sits on a rich man's lap
but grabs the throat of the pauper. -Danish

All water flows into the ocean or into the purse of the rich. -Danish

Honesty makes you rich, but she works slowly. -German

Everyone wipes his feet on poverty. -German

When a poor man eats a chicken, one or the other is sick. -Yiddish

Poverty generates resourcefulness. -Russian

Poverty is a sort of leprosy. -French

Poverty is the mother of all arts and trades. -English

Riches are gotten with pain, kept with care, and lost with grief. -English

Many by wit purchase wealth, but none by wealth purchase wit. -English

Settle one difficulty, and
you keep a hundred
others away. -Chinese

Slander by the stream will
be heard by the frogs. -Bantu

Silence is more than just a
lack of words. -Egyptian

Once you have decided to hit someone, then hit them hard because the
retribution will be the same whether
you hit hard or not. -Arabian

People live with their own id-
iosyncrasies and die of their
own illnesses. -Vietnamese

On the day of victory no
fatigue is felt. -Egyptian

Pearls are of no value in a desert.
-Indian

Set a beggar on horseback and
he'll run his horse to death.
-English

Only by falling do you learn
how to mount a horse. -Kurdish

Only when you have crossed
the river, can you say the
crocodile has a lump on his
snout. -Ghanian

A difficult case is difficult to answer. -Ghanian

Eternity gives no answer. -Jabo

Every saying or question has its appropriate answer. -Ghanian

If a case is greater than your wisdom and you give an answer to it,
you usually don't get the right solutions to it. -Ghanian

The fool has his answer on the edge of his tongue. -Egyptian

The mouth knows what it will say, not what it will be answered. -Hausa

When the child asked, "How do you hold the shield?",
the father answered, "The shield itself will teach you in war." -Oromo

For news of the heart ask the face. -Guinean

Silence is the best answer to the stupid. -Egyptian

When you go to someone's house and find him fighting
with his wife, don't be in a hurry to find an answer
for there is a reason why they are fighting. -Ghanian

Words are silver, but answers are gold. -Swahili

You don't ask for the food-box of someone who died of starvation -Ghanian

If the hide of an animal is rotten, you don't ask about the liver. -Ghanian

Tear off the curtain of doubt by questions. -Egyptian

The person you cannot overcome, do not ask to wrestle. -Oromo

A leopard is chasing us and do you ask me, "Is it a male or a female?" -Ghanian

When a dog is around one does not ask, "Who farted?" -Oromo

When one river is crossed they ask about
the other one they intend to cross. -Oromo

When the hunter comes from the bush carrying mushrooms,
he is not asked for news of his hunting. -Ashanti

Where the chief walks, there questions are decided. -Ovambo

145

By constantly asking, one can reach China. -Iranian

Ask the banker about gold, the jeweler about gems. -Turkish

The believer asks no questions,
while no answer can satisfy the unbeliever. -Hebrew

If you do not ask their help, all men are good natured. -Chinese

One must ask the delight of opium from one that smokes it. -Turkish

If you are offered a bull, do not ask how much milk he will give. -Arabian

If a dog offers to help you across the river,
don't ask if he is suffering from the mange. -Arabian

An answer that does not resolve a quarrel makes
a thousand new ones. -Chinese

Ask the experienced rather than the Learned.
-Arabian

A bird does not sing because he has the answer to something,
he sings because he has a song. -Chinese

Never has a man more need of his intelligence
than when a fool asks him a question. -Chinese

Don't promise something when you are full of joy;
don't answer letters when you are full of anger. -Chinese

The wise man asks questions of himself; the fool questions others. -Chinese

When the sculptor is dead his statues ask him for a soul. -Indian

If you wish to know the road ahead, inquire of those
who have traveled it. -Chinese

Going into a country, ask what is forbidden; on entering a village, ask what
are the customs; on entering a house, ask what should not be mentioned.
-Chinese

One idiot can ask more questions than ten wise men can answer. -Mongolian

A man finds joy in giving an apt reply—
and how good is a timely word! -Biblical

Answer a fool according to his folly,
or he will be wise in his own eyes. -Biblical

146

A well made remark gets no answer. -Iranian

He that asks faintly begs a denial. -English

Courteous asking breaks even city walls. -Russian

When the demand is a jest, the answer is a scoff. -English

The master does not ask the donkey if he may load him. -Serbo-Croatian

By asking the impossible you will get the best. -Italian

Even silence is an answer. -Romanian

To ask is no sin, and to be refused is no calamity. -Russian

Hasty questions require slow answers. -Dutch

Act honestly, and answer **boldly.** -Danish

Ask a lot, but take what is offered. -Russian

Never ask of him who has, but of him who wishes you well. -Spanish

To every answer you can find a new question. -Yiddish

A well-timed reply is worth its weight in gold. -Maltese

The winter asks you what you have done during the summer. -Latvian

The shortest answer is doing. -English

In a deal there are two fools: the one who asks too much and
the one who asks too little. -Russian

Truth gives a short answer, lies go around about. -German

If one has nothing to answer, it is best to shut up. -Yiddish

Every question requires not an answer. -English

Who says little has little to answer for. -German

He who has named his child 'stop
fighting' does not make bullets.
-Ghanian

She who needs a thing will travel
on a bad road to get it. -Ghanian

She who never has enough,
never has anything. -Spanish

He who has learned how to
steal, must learn how to hang.
-Malaysian

He who has daughters is
always a shepherd. -French

She who loves the truth
has many enemies. -Tamil

He who has got something
in his eyes cannot take it out
himself. -Ghanian

She who never begins will
never end. -Italian

She who makes the first
bad move always loses
the game. -Japanese

He who has an egg in his
pocket does not dance.
-Gabonese

The moon moves slowly, but it gets across the town. -Ghanian

Idleness moves so slowly that it will be overtaken by misery. -Madagascan

Even a slow walker will arrive. -Ovambo

Slowly but surely the excrement of foreign poets will come to your village. -Mali

Be a dog ever so quick to start
it will not catch a monkey swarming up a tree. -Fulani

The slow gait of a tortoise takes him far. -Swahili

If you skin the tiny ant slowly you can see its intestines. -Ghanian

The chameleon says: speed is good, and slowness is good. -Ghanian

If something is lying near the edge of the roof, pick it up quickly,
and don't let it fall down before doing so. -Ghanian

A person who is slow in eating can be seen
by his protruding hip bones. -Ghanian

Slowness is sometimes more advantageous that speed -Ghanian

Had I known my mother would die, I would have
gone to Accra and returned quickly. -Ghanian

The palm tree grub slowly eats away the palm tree. -Ghanian

You go to war slowly. -Ghanian

News is like a bird, it flies quickly. -Ghanian

We go quickly where we are sent when we take interest in the journey. -Wolof

If you are going to carry an animal, do it quickly,
don't let him make himself dirty before you carry him. -Ghanian

If you do something, do it quickly,
for my foot is stepping on the cutlass. -Ghanian

The deeds of God are done slowly. -Oromo

The old pot sweetens and quickly boils water. -Oromo

149

Caution brings speed in the end. -Hebrew

Good friends settle their accounts speedily. -Chinese

Working slowly produces fine goods. -Chinese

In bad things be slow; in good things be quick. -Afghan

What is not urgent must be done quickly
in order to take care of the urgent things calmly. -Chinese

As soon as a man leaves his house he has seven enemies. -Japanese

What is now top of the mast, will be firewood soon. -Burmese

Time flies away as fast as a shuttle on the loom. -Vietnamese

Both the fast and the slow will meet each other on the ferry boat. -Arabian

If you want to travel fast use the old roads. -Vietnamese

A cord of three strands is not quickly broken. -Biblical

Deep waters flow slowly. -Chinese

Be not afraid of going slowly, be afraid only of standing still. -Chinese

There are three things that have to be done quickly: burying the dead,
opening the door for a stranger, and fixing your daughter's wedding. -Iranian

Slow fires will smolder for a long time. -Thai

Easily promised, quickly forgotten. -Japanese

A day in prison is longer than a thousand years at large. -Vietnamese

The water of even the great ocean comes from one drop at a time. -Japanese

Gradually from chippings a mountain is made. -Kashmiri

The tongue slays quicker than the sword. -Turkish

The day we fear hastens toward us, the day we long for creeps. -Swedish

Drive slowly, you will get farther. -Estonian

One is not so soon healed as hurt. -English

The horses of hope gallop, but the asses of experience go slowly. -Russian

Dress slowly when you are in a hurry. -French

A forbidden meal is quickly eaten. -Swedish

Half a nose is quickly blown. -Danish

Age does not give you good sense, it only makes you go slowly. -Finnish

If you fail to practice your art, it will soon disappear. -German

What is well done is done **soon enough.**

-English

Slowly but surely the bird builds his nest. -Dutch

The slower you go, the farther you will be. -Russian

A tale is soon told; a deed is not soon done. -Russian

On your own donkey it is quicker than on someone else's racehorse.
-Yugoslavian

Roses and maidens soon lose their bloom. -German

Speed and accuracy do not agree. -Irish

The highest spoke in fortune's wheel may soon turn lowest. -English

Large trees grow slowly and fall suddenly. -Serbo-Croatian

Dry wood makes a quick fire. -Danish

Spending is quick, earning is slow. -Russian

The death throes of an elephant are
not so annoying as a living flea.
-Zanzibari

The church is near, but the way
is icy. The tavern is far, but I
will walk carefully. -Ukrainian

The crocodile does not die under the
water so that we can call the monkey to celebrate its funeral. -Nigerian

Stay till the lame messenger
come, if you will know the
truth of the thing. -English

The ball always looks for the
best player. -French

Some men will build a wine
cellar when they have found
just one grape. -Lebanese

The anvil lasts longer than the
hammer. -Italian

The buffalo which comes late will
have to drink muddy water and
eat dried grass. -Vietnamese

Taking water from the same
well doesn't make all the wives'
gravy taste good. -Ivorian

The account of the donkey is different from the account of the
donkey-man. -Turkish

Do not regret that which passed; do not forget
that which is coming. -Oromo

Forgetfulness is like being tripped up. -Basotho

One who recovers from sickness, forgets about God. -Ethiopian

The buttocks that forget, the black ants bite twice. -Oromo

When a cock gets drunk it forgets about the hawk. -Ghanian

The wrongdoer forgets, but not the wronged. -African

They ate our food, and forgot our names. -Tunisian

What you have not seen you don't remember. -Ghanian

To **trouble me** is better than to **forget me.** -African

The ax forgets but the cut log does not. -Shona

Forgetting is the cure for suffering. -Swahili

The little promise you promised is not forgotten. -Bemba

No person who dies is completely forgotten. -Oromo

A dog never forgets his master. -African

A guest who breaks the dishes of his host is not soon forgotten. -African

Work is good provided you do not forget to live. -Bantu

The eye never forgets what the heart has seen. -Bantu

The person who goes to toilet in the bush here and there
should remember where he has gone previously. -Ghanian

Victory is a thing that is remembered. -Fulani

The wife forgot her husband but she remembered to
collect her big potatoes. -Oromo

153

Knowledge acquired in childhood is not soon forgotten. -Hebrew

Do not forget little kindnesses and do not remember small faults. -Chinese

The ink of a scholar is worth as much as the martyr's blood. -Islamic

There is no remembrance of men of old, and even those who are
yet to come will not be remembered by those who follow. -Biblical

Mankind is made out of forgetfulness. -Arabian

A mule can swim seven different strokes
but the moment he sees the water he forgets them all. -Armenian

The wise man forgets insults as the ungrateful forget benefits. -Chinese

Liars are forgetful. -Iranian

When the pain has passed one forgets the medicine. -Vietnamese

When the knife is over a man's head, he remembers GOD. -Pashtun

To see a man do a good deed is to forget all his faults. -Chinese

An old horse does not forget his path. -Japanese

In the hour of distress, a vow; in the hour of release, forgetfulness. -Hebrew

When the new is there, the old is forgotten. -Vietnamese

There are five ways in which to become wise: be silent, listen, remember,
grow older and study. -Arabian

To forget one's ancestors is to be a brook without a source,
a tree without a root. -Chinese

It is easy to forget a kindness, but one remembers unkindness. -Indian

When eating bamboo sprouts, remember the man who planted them. -Chinese

Keep a dog for three days and he will not forget your kindness,
but three years kindness shown to a cat is forgotten in three days. -Japanese

In peace do not forget war. -Japanese

Memory is the treasure of the mind. -English

If you are in the house of a friend, bad times are soon forgotten. -Albanian

Prices are forgotten, quality remains. -French

The less you know, the less you forget. -Norwegian

When he mounts his horse he forgets God; when he dismounts,
he forgets his horse. -Russian

Butterflies forget that they were once caterpillars. -Swedish

When a musician has forgotten his note, he makes as though
a crumb stuck in his throat. -English

Nothing is so new as what has long been forgotten. -German

What was hard to endure is sweet to recall. -French

Pain is forgotten where gain follows. -English

Strangers forgive, friends forget. -Slovenian

When a toothache comes, you forget your headache. -Yiddish

A Christian forgives, an idiot forgets. -Corsican

To want to forget something is to remember it. -French

Experience is the father of wisdom, and memory the mother. -English

Better twice remembered than once forgotten. -German

When you are right no one remembers;
when you are wrong no one forgets. -Irish

The last benefit is most remembered. -English

What you learn to your cost you remember long. -Danish

God delays, but never forgets. -Greek

She who predicts the future lies, even if she tells the truth. -Arabian

She who rides a camel should not be afraid of dogs. -Berber

He who gets a name for early rising can stay in bed until midday. -Irish

He who goes out on a journey without a guide loses his way. -Turkish

She who possesses patience, possesses all things. -Yoruba

He who has a dog need not bark himself. -Norwegian

He who goes out to the chase without a greyhound comes home without a hare. -Turkish

She who paddles two canoes, sinks. -Bemba

He who guards himself will not perish. -Ovambo

She who plants thistles does not reap grapes. -Lebanese

One day in perfect health is much. -Egyptian

There is no doctor on the day of death. -Fulani

The physician's fee is not paid till the sickness is over. -Ashanti

Health is a crown and no one knows it save a sick person. -Swahili

If there is neither food nor drink, plain water is medicine. -Hausa

There is no medicine against old age. -Yoruba

There is no medicine to cure hatred. -Ghanian

Health of the body is prosperity. -Hausa

There is no cure that does not have its price. -Kenyan

If you want to give a sick man medicine, let him first be really ill—
so that he can see how well the medicine works. -Nigerian

When you are sick you promise a goat,
but when you are well again make do with a chicken. -Nigerian

To a physician a sick man is a garden. -Swahili

A physician does not drink medicine for the sick. -Ga

Death is the pursuer, disease the constant companion of man. -Madagascan

You cannot buy the power of healing diseases. -Ghanian

Daytime is medicine. -Basotho

Even though an old man is strong and healthy, he won't live forever. -Ghanian

Disease gradually heals, trouble gradually goes away. -Oromo

She hid her sickness and died without medicine. -Oromo

When the sore is healed, flies go away. -Basotho

157

Diseases enter by the mouth, misfortunes issue from it. -Chinese

When the disease is not known there is no remedy. -Burmese

Fasting is the best medicine. -Hindi

Those who suffer from the same illness pity each other. -Korean

There is no such thing as tasty medicine. -Hebrew

When the heart is at ease, the body is healthy. -Chinese

Even an accomplished physician cannot cure himself. -Chinese

Wine tops the list of all medicines. -Hebrew

Sometimes the body becomes healthy by being very sick. -Iranian

Victims of the same disease have a lot to talk about.
-Japanese

When fate strikes physicians are useless. -Iranian

Man is the instrument of illness. -Japanese

There is no cure for an unknown illness. -Burmese

Too many doctors caused the boy's death. -Burmese

Only the cure you believe in cures. -Tamil

The physician prescribes the medicine, the vulture waits for the body. -Turkish

Whatever a physician prescribes is a remedy. -Tamil

Adapt the remedy to the disease. -Chinese

As fallow soil gives birth to weeds, old age gives birth to disease. -Vietnamese

A cheerful heart is good medicine, but a crushed spirit dries up the bones.
-Biblical

The chamber of sickness is the chapel of devotion. -English

Desperate diseases must have desperate cures. -English

A great doctor is accompanied by a great angel. -Yiddish

He that eats till he is sick must fast till he is well. -English

God heals and the doctor gets the money. -Flemish

Illness comes by many roads but always uninvited. -Czech

Illness gives you the taste of health. -Hungarian

Nature, time, and patience are the three great physicians. -English

A doctor and a clown know more than a doctor alone. -Italian

Sickness comes in like a horse and leaves like a snail. -French

Every doctor thinks his pills are the best. -French

The doctor is often more to be feared than the disease. -French

The rich have medicines the poor have health. -German

Time, not medicine, cures the sick. -Portuguese

The medicine that hurts the most is generally the best healer. -Scottish

Limit your desires and you will improve your health. -Spanish

What cures the liver harms the spleen. -Spanish

Don't settle in a place where the doctor has gout. -Yiddish

The strong man's sport is the sickly man's death. -German

The world holds more for the healthy than the wealthy. -Slovakian

The jug goes to the well until it gets broken; the wolf goes to the herd until he gets killed.
-Estonian

The key that opens is also the key that locks. -African

The knife for flaying an elephant needs not size but sharpness.
-Hausa

The goal will not be reached if the right distance not be traveled. -Tibetan

The hunter in pursuit of an elephant does not stop to throw stones at birds. -Ugandan

The dragon teaches you that if you want to climb high you have to do it against the wind.
-Chinese

The dust raised by the sheep does not choke the wolf.
-English

The end of the pig is the beginning of the sausage.
-Italian

The first half of life is spent in longing for the second, the second half in regretting the first. -French

The dog who has a wound on its buttocks does not sit as it wishes.
-Oromo

If the music changes so does the dance. -Hausa

If everyone is going to dance, who, then, would watch? -Cameroonian

Singing "Alleluia" everywhere does not prove piety. -Ethiopian

You cannot dance well on only one leg. -Bantu

If you can't dance well, you'd better not get up. -Nigerois

Even the fall of a dancer is a somersault. -Wolof

If the song doesn't sound well, you don't imitate its tune. -Ghanian

If you make a mistake in the beginning, you can't lead the dance. -Ghanian

No one pays for someone's Dancing; the Dance pays for itself.
-Ghanian

Whistling causes people to sing. -Ghanian

If the singing and dance is good we will even crawl to see it. -Ghanian

If you visit a place and hear children singing songs, these songs are the very ones sung by their ancestors and handed down to the children. -Ghanian

Even if the drum does not sound well, you dance to it all the same. -Ghanian

If you don't know how to dance, you say you don't like the sound of the drum. -Ghanian

A dancer is always stimulated to dance when the drums are beaten. -Ghanian

The leader of the song does not sing. -Lugbara

The poor person who obtained prosperity will dance with the handle of an axe. -Oromo

What you don't have don't sing about. -Oromo

When the hero sings, the one who failed looks at the ground. -Oromo

Whistling does not come from the mouth when there is no song in the heart. -Nkundu-Mongo

The temple girl who could not dance
said that the hall was not large enough. -Tamil

The soul of an idiot is always dancing on the end of his tongue. -Arabian

Heavenly music is interpreted differently by everyone. -Chinese

Keep a green tree In your heart and perhaps
the singing bird will come. -Chinese

There are many people who can sing, but don't know the words. -Indian

If you beat my drum, I will blow your whistle. -Lebanese

The bear knows seven songs and they are all about honey. -Turkish

A Wedding is like a funeral, but with musicians. -Hebrew

You will hate a beautiful song if you sing it often. -Korean

The tone of the bird's song is the same everywhere. -Japanese

Although shrimps may dance around they do not leave the river. -Japanese

As the drum beats, so goes the dance. -Malaysian

The mosque is no place to dance. -Iranian

Music has no charms for a buffalo. -Bihar

Talk of music only to a musician. -Chinese

To sing to the deaf, to talk with the dumb, and to dance
for the blind are three foolish things. -Indian

We played the flute for you, and you did not dance;
we sang a dirge, and you did not mourn. -Biblical

Look at the book and sing as it directs. -Chinese

There is a time to mourn and a time to dance. -Biblical

Sing his praise who gives you food. -Bihar

If the bride can't dance, she finds fault with the musicians. -Yiddish

Dance alone and you can jump all you wish. -Greek

If you're sitting on his cart you must sing his song. -Russian

Not every one that dances is glad. -French

In the fiddler's house every one is a dancer. -French

The willing dancer is easily played to. -Hungarian

To a bad dancer even the hem of her skirt will be in the way. -Polish

You can cage a bird but you can't make it sing. -French

Birds of prey do not sing. -German

Necessity teaches even the lame to dance. -German

The cripple is always the one to open the dancing. -Austrian

Every story has two sides and every song has twelve versions. -Icelandic

From a broken violin do not expect fine music. -Greek

Stay where there are songs. Bad people don't sing. -Gypsy

There is more to dancing than a pair of dancing shoes. -Dutch

When we sing everybody hears us, when we sigh nobody hears us. -Russian

To every new song one can find an old tune. -Yiddish

If you dance at every wedding, you'll weep at every funeral. -Yiddish

Music helps not the toothache. -English

Great strokes make not sweet music. -English

She who seems to be for
you may be working
against you. -Ghanian

She who sees death, con-
sents to sickness. -Turkish

He who eats when he is full digs
his grave with his teeth. -Turkish

She who rides the horse of
greed at a gallop will pull it up
at the door of shame. -Fulani

She who runs from the white
ant may stumble upon the
stinging ant. -Nigerian

He who finds a wife finds what is
good and receives favor from the
LORD. -Biblical

He who farms is spared
the trouble of buying
corn. -Hausa

He who enters the tavern,
enters not to say his prayers.
-Romanian

He who excuses himself accuses
himself. -French

She who rises early finds the
way short. -Wolof

The father's friend is no friend of the son. -Fulani

Everybody loves a fool, but nobody wants him for a son. -Ivorian

Poverty is an older daughter of laziness. -Wolof

The crab's daughter does not bear a bird. -Oji

Honey is the daughter of the bee. -Lugbara

A mother will not listen to the crying of her married daughter. -Oromo

First they look at the mother, then they marry the daughter. -Oromo

If the chief hates you he marries your daughter.
-Ghanian

The daughter advises her mother about childbirth. -Oromo

The mother acts on what she learnt, the daughter on what she saw. -Oromo

When they like the mother, they kiss the daughter. -Oromo

A son is the bone of hard times. -Ovambo

The son disgraces his father by bad conduct. -Efik

If the son of the chief wants abuse, he'll get it. -Ghanian

Ananse's son, Ntikuma, does not go and sleep under the tree
which killed his father. -Ghanian

If your mother is alive, you are not called your father's son. -Ghanian

A son may run past his father but will never be ahead of him. -Oromo

Rather than begetting a bad son it is better to beget
a good girl and depend on a son-in-law. -Oromo

The mother said to her blind son, "Morning star of mine;"
and to her lame son, "Straight river of mine." -Oromo

The mother who is a thief does not trust her daughter. -Oromo

165

Though a king, he is the son of his mother. -Tamil

It is easier to govern a country than a son. -Chinese

With a good son-in-law you gain a son, with a bad one
you lose your daughter, too. -Hebrew

Vinegar is the son of wine. -Hebrew

Why save when your son is a good son?
Why save when your son is a bad son? -Indian

A spoiled son becomes a gambler,
while a spoiled daughter becomes a harlot. -Indian

Only two things matter in this world: a son and a daughter. -Indian

If you love your son, make him leave home. -Japanese

An ungrateful son is a wart on his father's nose—
he leaves it, it's ugly, he removes it, it hurts. -Iranian

In a house where there are many beautiful daughters
the soup kettle will never get polished. -Manchurian

Your five year old son is your instructor; at ten your slave;
at fifteen your equal and after that either friend or foe. -Turkish

When the father has eaten too much salt in his lifetime,
then his son thereafter will have a great thirst. -Vietnamese

To raise a son without learning is raising an ass;
to raise a daughter without learning is raising a pig. -Chinese

My son, if sinners entice you, do not give in to them. -Biblical

Daughters are fragile ware. -Japanese

See the mother, comprehend the daughter. -Pashtun

Truth is the daughter of the gods. -Japanese

No wise man takes responsibility
for an eighteen-year-old daughter. -Chinese

Your son can be a prince, your daughter will be a mother. -Kurdish

If there is only one earring among seven daughters,
there will always be a quarrel on festival days. -Tibetan

The Rabbi's daughter is forbidden what the bathhouse keeper's daughter is allowed. -Yiddish

I give a present to the mother but I think of the daughter. -German

When Anger and Revenge get married, their daughter is called Cruelty. -Russian

When a father gives to his son, they both laugh. When a son gives to his father, they both weep. -Yiddish

Happy is she who marries the son of a dead mother. -Scottish

The son of an ass brays twice a day. -Spanish

A son-in-law never becomes a son and a daughter-in-law never quite becomes a daughter. -Greek

One good daughter is worth **seven sons.** -Russian

Truth is the daughter of time. -English

Wonder is the daughter of ignorance. -English

Walk straight, my son—as the old crab said to the young crab. -Irish

After all, every man is the son of a woman. -Russian

A miserly father makes a prodigal son. -French

Better be a poor man's son than the slave of a rich. -Romanian

The magistrate's son gets out of every scrape. -Spanish

When the daughter dies, the son-in-law is dead as well. -French

Daughters are easy to rear, but hard to marry. -German

Marry your son when you will, your daughter when you can. -Danish

Ingratitude is the daughter of pride. -English

A girl with a golden cradle doesn't remain long in her father's house. -Armenian

167

The thumb cannot point
straight forwards. -Yoruba

The twig that falls in the water will
never become a fish. -Ivorian

The tree that is not taller than
you cannot shade you. -African

The nail supports the hoof,
the hoof the horse,
the horse the man, the man
the world. -Arabian

The prettiest of shoes makes
a sorry hat. -Japanese

The market of debauch
is always open. -Egyptian

The place to get top speed out of
a horse is not the place where you
can get top speed out of a canoe.
-Hausa

The shoe should fit the foot and
not the foot the shoe. -Greek

The needs of the monkey are not
those of the anteater. -Fulani

The path of duty lies in what is
near at hand, but men look for
it in what is remote. -Japanese

Guile excels strength. -Hausa

The thrower of stones throws away the strength of his own arm. -African

Even a weak lion is not bitten by a dog. -Bantu

The lion's power lies in our fear of him. -Nigerian

If the stomach be not strong, do not eat cockroaches. -Yoruba

The strength of a fish is in the water. -Shona

The strength of one person only does not go far. -Bemba

The multitude is stronger than the king. -Tunisian

If someone hits you on the top of your head,
he is making your neck strong. -Ghanian

However strong you are, you don't do the work of two men. -Ghanian

A debtor has no strength. -Ghanian

The strength of the worn hoe comes from the owner. -Lugbara

A strong bull they overcome while it limps. -Oromo

A weak person loves the weakness of the strong. -Oromo

One strong man does not catch another strong man. -Ghanian

If the large rubber tree dies
it is because of the strong vines growing on it. -Ghanian

Too much strength brings trouble. -Ghanian

If you keep pulling, it breaks. -Ghanian

He fought heartily but lacked strength. -Oromo

The heart is diligent, but the body is weak. -Basotho

169

Even the ant has his bite. -Turkish

The voice of a poor man does not carry very far. -Laotian

You know a man by the sweat of his brow
and the strength of his word.
-Arabian

Two weaklings conquered the fort. -Arabian

Distance tests a horses strength; time reveals a man's character. -Chinese

If a man becomes powerful even his chicken and his dog
go to heaven. -Chinese

If you are not so strong, don't carry heavy burdens.
If your words are worthless, don't give advice. -Chinese

Great souls have wills; feeble ones have only wishes. -Chinese

The power of the stream comes from the source. -Iranian

Under a powerful general there are no feeble soldiers. -Japanese

A powerful man has big ears. -Japanese

Only he who knows his own weaknesses can endure those of others.
-Japanese

The talkers aren't strong; the strong don't talk. -Burmese

A man's spirit sustains him in sickness,
but a crushed spirit who can bear? -Biblical

If you falter in times of trouble, how small is your strength! -Biblical

I have seen something else under the sun: The race is not to the swift or the
battle to the strong... but time and chance happen to them all. -Biblical

It is a sign of weakness just to let things happen. -Arabian

The spirit is willing, but the flesh is weak. -Biblical

Men know not their own faults; oxen know not their own strength. -Chinese

Weaklings never forgive their enemies. -Chinese

Chains of gold are stronger than chains of iron. -English

Would you be strong, conquer yourself. -German

The angry and the weak are their own enemies. -Russian

One good head is better than a hundred strong hands. -English

Man is sometimes stronger than iron and at other times
weaker than a fly. -Yiddish

The strongest among the weak is the one who doesn't forget
his weaknesses. -Danish

Unanimity is the strongest fortress. -Danish

A **good cause**
makes a stout heart
and a strong arm. -English

If the ox knew his own strength. God help us. -Greek

Time has strong teeth. -Norwegian

Always be patient with the rich and powerful. -Spanish

A hungry wolf is stronger than a satisfied dog. -Ukrainian

You do not fall because you are weak, you fall because
you think you are strong. -Yiddish

What is play to the strong is death to the weak. -Danish

As the years go by, the teeth and the memory grow weaker. -Yiddish

Better weak beer than an empty cask. -Danish

Strong folks have strong maladies. -German

Pull gently at a weak rope. -Dutch

Willows are weak, yet they bind other wood. -English

Once you're taken on the yoke,
don't say that you're not strong enough. -Russian

She who shoots often hits
at last. -German

She who sits in the
shade won't take an
axe to the tree. -Japanese

She who shares the meat is
always left with the bone.
-Laplandish

She who sells cheap, sells
quickly. -Turkish

He who dreads fire, guards
himself even from smoke.
-Turkish

He who doesn't go to war roars
like a lion. -Iranian

He who does not regularly put
on clean socks will never get
used to circus life. -Chinese

He who does not teach his
son a trade teaches him to
steal. -Hebrew

He who doesn't like chat-
tering women must stay a
bachelor. -Congolese

She who sells the ox sets its
price. -French

The one who listens is the one who understands. -Jabo

Everything the mouth says, it does not do. -Kpelle

I am talking to you, daughter-in-law,
so that you could hear it, neighbor! -Egyptian

Advise and counsel him; if he does not listen,
let adversity teach him. -Ethiopian

"If it is not a boy it will be a girl," says the fortuneteller. -Madagascan

What the child says, he has heard at home. -Nigerian

The quarrel that doesn't concern you is pleasant to hear about. -Hausa

A good talk is like beads that are beautifully strung.
-Ghanian

However sweet talk, silence is better. -Fulani

What women say is nonsense; but he who does not listen in is a fool. -Bemba

Do not say the first thing that comes to your mind. -Kenyan

If you come near the river, you will hear the crab cough. -Ghanian

I know how to shout a curse, but the thief is hard of hearing. -Ghanian

It is through your eyes that you hear what is being said. -Ghanian

She refused to listen and was annoyed when they kicked her. -Oromo

Talkativeness is a misfortune. -Ghanian

Man finishes eating but not talking. -Ghanian

Because of talking it became an issue;
because of scratching it became a rash. -Oromo

If one talks about everything the heart remains empty. -Oromo

They will never be short of things to talk about and to burn. -Oromo

173

A drum beaten on a hill is heard far and wide. -Chinese

A general of a defeated army should not talk of tactics. -Japanese

The whisper of a pretty girl can be heard
further off than the roar of a lion. -Arabian

There is gossip every day,
but if no one listens anymore the gossip will die. -Chinese

With money you can make the dead speak; without it
you can't even keep the deaf quiet. -Chinese

You always win by not saying the things you don't have to say. -Chinese

When people only talk about things they understand
then a great silence will descend upon the world. -Chinese

Talking without thinking is shooting without aiming. -Chinese

Teach your tongue to say:
"I do not know." -Hebrew

It is better to talk to a woman and think of God,
than talk to God and think of a woman. -Hebrew

At harvest time the gardener is deaf. -Iranian

A silent man is the best one to listen to. -Japanese

Even the best song becomes tiresome if heard too often. -Korean

If you talk to the blacksmith you'll get hit by sparks. -Kurdish

The more you listen the more you give yourself room for doubt. -Mongolian

To listen to a lie is harder than to tell it. -Turkish

When a thing is done, don't talk about it. -Chinese

Don't give an order after listening only to one side. -Japanese

If you don't hear the story clearly, don't carry it off with you
under your arm. -Thai

Do not be quick with your mouth, do not be hasty in your heart
to utter anything before God. -Biblical

Every ass loves to hear himself bray. -English

A full belly is deaf to learning. -Russian

Each bird loves to hear himself sing. -English

One must talk soothingly to the dog until one has passed him. -French

He is a fool that praises himself,
and he is a madman that speaks ill of himself. -Danish

Hear twice before you speak once. -English

All that is said in the kitchen should not be heard in the parlor. -Scottish

A good listener makes a good teacher. -Polish

Two **great talkers** never go far together. -Spanish

If you want to hear the truth about yourself—offend your neighbor. -Czech

It is useless to knock at the door of a deaf man. -Greek

Listen to that which is well said even if it is from
the mouth of an enemy. -Greek

Children will tell you what they do, men what they think
and older people what they have seen and heard. -Gypsy

Much talk, little work. -Dutch

Once a word has been uttered it belongs to those who hear it. -Montenegrin

If God listened to every shepherd's curse,
our sheep would all be dead. -Russian

Talking about bulls is altogether different from being in the arena. -Spanish

Don't talk too much, because your ignorance
is greater than your knowledge. -Spanish

A deaf man heard how a mute told that
a blind man saw how a cripple walked. -Yiddish

175

It is easier to hear a secret than to keep it. -Yiddish

The vulture scents the carcass,
however high in the air he may be.
-Yoruba

They don't unload the caravan for
one lame donkey. -Iranian

Those who live together cannot hide
their behinds from each other. -Ovambo

The water dog chews on the fishing
net, but he doesn't tear up the ears
of a rat to pay for it. -Ghanian

Those who inherit fortunes are
frequently more of a problem than
those who made them. -Congolese

The vulture's body is a foolish looking
thing, yet even he does not eat with
someone who doesn't bathe. -Ghanian

There's not enough if there's
not too much. -French

Thorns themselves will not
harm you—you hurt yourself
on the thorns. -African

The water of the river flows on
without waiting for the thirsty
man. -Kenyan

The world has not made a
promise to anybody. -African

Treat the days well and they will treat you well. -Bemba

No matter how long a log floats on the river,
it will never be a crocodile. -Bambara

No matter how long the winter, spring is sure to follow. -Guinean

Time destroys all things. -Nigerian

He ate one fig and he thought the autumn had come. -Tunisian

Rather than resembling one's father, resembling the times is better. -Oromo

One result of sin comes quickly, one gradually. -Oromo

Eat when the meal is ready, speak when the time is ripe. -Ethiopian

No matter how long the night, the day is sure to come. -Congolese

Wherever there is much talking the dawn doesn't come quickly. -Ghanian

In times of poverty, we marry a hunchbacked person. -Ghanian

The guest is a guest, even if he stays a winter or a summer. -Moroccan

The vegetables that are not ripe during the okro season
have their own season. -Ghanian

When the rainy season sets in, you can't avoid house flies. -Ghanian

For the rainy season that will come next year
one thatches the roof this year. -Oromo

The person whom God has cursed trades butter in the hot season,
and salt in the rainy season. -Oromo

The water that was helpful in the dry season they curse in the rainy season.
-Oromo

In time 'Twenty years hence' becomes 'tomorrow.' -Yoruba

The year is far off, the year is far off, but it arrives at last. -Ghanian

177

The roast takes a long time to a hungry man. -Hausa

Though the camel go to Mecca forty years
he does not become a pilgrim. -Turkish

You raise flowers for a year; you see them for but ten days. -Chinese

A fat woman is a blanket for the winter. -Arabian

Just because men do not like the cold.
Heaven will not stop the winter. -Chinese

There is a time to fish and a time to dry the nets. -Chinese

The harvest of a whole year depends on what you
sow in the springtime. -Chinese

Sometimes it takes only an hour to get a reputation
that lasts for a thousand years. -Japanese

The poor have no time to spare. -Japanese

You warm up something for ten days and it goes cold in one. -Japanese

There is a time for everything,
and a season for every activity under heaven. -Biblical

Every spring has an autumn and every road an ending. -Iranian

Years and months are like a flowing stream. -Japanese

Dogs become mad only during one season of the year,
but man is foolish all the year around. -Vietnamese

Never leave your field in spring or your house in winter. -Chinese

A man's heart is as changeable as the skies in autumn. -Japanese

With the fall of one leaf we know
that autumn has come to the world. -Japanese

There is not a single season without fruit. -Turkish

A single kind word keeps one warm for three winters. -Chinese

Those who are happy do not observe how time goes by. -Chinese

Time flies like an arrow, once gone it does not return. -Japanese

One blossom doesn't make a spring. -Armenian

The days follow each other and are not alike. -French

A fence lasts three years, a dog lasts three fences, a horse three dogs,
and a man three horses. -German

In the garden of time grows the flower of consolation. -Russian

A whore in spring, a nun in autumn. -Catalonian

Keep a thing seven years and you'll find a use for it. -Gaelic

If you do not sow in the spring you will not reap in the autumn. -Irish

You can do nothing about governments and winter. -Slovenian

Feed a **wolf** in the **winter** and he will **devour you** in the **summer.** -Greek

A hundred years hence we shall all be bald. -Spanish

A life without love is like a year without summer. -Swedish

One summer's day is worth a whole week in winter. -Ukrainian

It is not enough to run; one must start in time. -French

From tomorrow till tomorrow time goes a long journey. -French

Time and money make everything possible. -Maltese

The winter sun is like a stepmother—
it shines, but does not warm. -Russian

Give time time. -Italian

Time brings wounds and heals them. -Yiddish

Every mile is two in winter. -English

Play in summer, starve in winter. -English

He who does not lose his way by
night will not lose his way by day.
-Nigerois

She who speaks much is sure
to talk nonsense. -Greek

He who does not open his
eyes must open his purse.
-German

He who does not know what
to do in his spare time is not a
businessman. -Chinese

She who sows well, reaps well. -Spanish

He who does not mend his clothes
will soon have none. -Nigerois

She who sows brambles must not
go barefoot. -Spanish

He who does not listen does
not sit at the council. -Bemba

She who stands still in
the mud sticks in it.
-Chinese

She who does not tire, achieves.
-Spanish

God does not hide a liar. -Swahili

If you want to know how the true story goes,
wait till the arguments start. -African

Believe the liar up to the door of his house and no further than that. -Egyptian

One falsehood spoils a thousand truths. -Ghanian

A false story has seven endings. -Swahili

Lies have short legs. -Lugbara

When you speak the truth in stating a case,
the matter is quickly settled. -Ghanian

Truth is a companion of God. -Oromo

Honesty is not always immediately evident. -Ghanian

Because one's hair is white one's word is not true. -Oromo

The Lord opens the gate for the truth. -Oromo

The person with dysentery cannot sleep; the person with truth cannot keep
silent. -Oromo

The truth that was lost in the morning comes home in the evening. -Oromo

Though the truth may become skinny it will never perish. -Oromo

Truth is the home to which one returns. -Oromo

The end of the ox is beef, and the end of a lie is exposure. -Madagascan

Who travels alone tells lies. -Oji

A man on his death bed tells no lies. -Swahili

Where talk is abundant, there a lie slips in. -Hausa

Truth is a lion, and lies are a hyena. -Moroccan

181

One man tells a falsehood, a hundred repeat it as true. -Chinese

Excuses are always mixed with lies. -Arabian

A fable is a bridge that leads to truth. -Arabian

When you shoot an arrow of truth, dip its point in honey. -Arabian

Whenever there is profit to be made then think of honesty. -Chinese

A good storyteller must be able to lie a little. -Chinese

If you add to the truth, you take something away from it. -Hebrew

Truth has no branches. -Indian

Lies will blossom but never bear fruit. -Iranian

A lie has no legs, but scandalous wings. -Japanese

If you tell the truth too early, you are laughed at
—too late and you are stoned. -Iranian

A joke is often the hole through which truth whistles. -Japanese

If you wish to learn the highest truth, begin with the alphabet. -Japanese

A dressed up lie is worth more than a badly told truth. -Lebanese

You can proclaim the truth also in a friendly way. -Turkish

To know the truth is easy; but, ah, how difficult to follow it! -Chinese

Falsehood is common, truth uncommon. -Hebrew

Don't burn false incense before a true god. -Chinese

A liar is the beginning of a thief. -Japanese

If a lie saves, truth is a surer savior. -Lebanese

A child, a drunkard, and a fool tell the truth. -Hungarian

A lie you must not tell; the truth you don't have to tell. -Yiddish

If lies were as heavy as stones to carry many would prefer the truth. -Swedish

One lie is a lie, two are lies, but three is politics! -Yiddish

Though a lie be swift, truth overtakes it. -Italian

With lies you will go far, but not back again. -Yiddish

To tell the truth is dangerous; to listen to it is boring. -Danish

To deceive a diplomat speak the truth, he has no experience with it. -Greek

A liar never believes anyone else. -Yiddish

There are such things as false truths and honest lies. -Gypsy

A little truth helps the lie go down. -Italian

In the lake of lies there are many dead fish. -Russian

Rather a bitter truth than a sweet lie. -Russian

There are many lies but barely one truth. -Ukrainian

Truth is the safest lie. -Yiddish

A thousand probabilities do not make one truth. -English

Singers, lovers, and poets lie a lot. -German

In too much dispute truth is lost. -English

The truth may walk around naked; the lie has to be clothed. -Yiddish

Truth lies at the bottom of a well. -English

To enjoy life is worth so much
more than it costs. -French

Though a cow yields three measures of milk, it is not desirable if it
pulls down the roof. -Tamil

To get milk and eggs you must not
frighten the cow and hen. -Tibetan

Though the bird may fly over your
head, let it not make its nest in
your hair. -Danish

Time causes remembrance. -Efik

Though small, a needle is not to
be swallowed. -Japanese

Three may keep a secret, if two
of them are dead. -English

Though the cow gives a large pot
of milk, it is not equal to the horse
in speed. -Tamil

To change one's habits has a
smell of death. -Portuguese

Though the hyena eats meat
it drops white crap. -Oromo

Don't join in a fight if you have no weapons. -Swahili

If we don't fight we remain equals,
if we do fight then one of us wins. -Madagascan

Courage is shown on the battlefield, not in the house. -Ghanian

If your part of the battlefield is in a difficult situation, you don't leave it
and go to where it is easy. -Ghanian

If a grown-up divides things, there is peace. -Ghanian

The means for pacification goes to the person before peace comes. -Ghanian

By saying: "Let it be," people remain together in peace. -Oromo

A **peacemaker often receives wounds.** -Yoruba

For you to spend the night in peace, your neighbor
must spend the night in peace. -Oromo

People who respect each other live in peace. -Oromo

Peace is prosperity. -Basotho

Those killed in war are not counted before the army has been defeated. -Ghanian

If you fight with your tongue only, you don't win a war. -Ghanian

If you fight, go forward, and you will win the battle. -Ghanian

If two men fight, the third one is the peacemaker. -Ghanian

If you are cooking the war medicine and there is a fire of untruth under it,
it will never be well cooked. -Ghanian

If spending your money gives you pain when you go to war,
you will not win. -Ghanian

A son goes out to war in the morning;
he comes home when God wills. -Oromo

They don't praise the army going to war, they praise it on returning. -Oromo

Living in peace is better than living as a king. -Hausa

The more you fight the more you get hurt. -Vietnamese

The grass suffers in the fight of the tiger and buffalo. -Bihar

Cavalry horses delight in battle. -Chinese

You may live in peace when your neighbors permit. -Hindi

An army of sheep led by a lion would defeat an army of lions led by a sheep. -Arabian

The tree of silence bears the fruits of peace. -Arabian

War is a disaster for winner and loser alike. -Arabian

The most useful holy war is the one fought against your own passions. -Arabian

The world exists on three things: truth, justice, and peace. -Hebrew

If peace reigns in the land, a nun can govern it. -Tibetan

A harvest of peace grows from seeds of contentment. -Indian

A fight in your neighbor's house is refreshing. -Indian

Thirty-six plans of how to win the battle are not so good as one plan to withdraw from the fight. -Japanese

A hundred men can sit together quietly but when two dogs get together there will be a fight. -Kurdish

When the healthy dog fights with a mad dog, it is the ears of the healthy one that are bitten off. -Burmese

There is no other happiness but peace. -Thai

Thunder will bring to a peaceful end a quarrel between husband and wife. -Japanese

In a fight between whales, the backs of shrimps are burst. -Korean

The soldiers fight, and the kings are heroes. -Hebrew

Better a dog in times of peace than a man in times of rebellion. -Chinese

Two are an army against one. -Icelandic

It takes two blows to make a battle. -English

Two dogs fight for a bone and a third runs away with it. -German

Better an egg in peace than an ox in war. -English

When the miller fights with the chimneysweep,
the miller becomes black and the chimneysweep white. -Yiddish

Money is the sinew of war. -English

A strong attack is half the battle won. -Basque

During the battle you cannot lend your sword to anyone. -Bosnian

Make peace with men, and quarrel with your sins. -Russian

One minute of **patience** can mean ten years of **peace.** -Greek

Better keep peace than make peace. -Dutch

Go early to market and as late as you can to battle. -Italian

Let war be waged in the house of him who wants it. -Serbo-Croatian

Love is like war: you begin when you like
and leave off when you can. -Spanish

If one soldier knew what the other thinks, there would be no war. -Yiddish

A bad peace is better than a good war. -Russian

For the sake of peace one may even lie. -Yiddish

Peace feeds, war wastes; peace breeds, war consumes. -Danish

You cannot have peace longer than your neighbor chooses. -Danish

Water in peace is better than wine in war. -German

She who told you that the liver of the bush cow is delicious should not be left out when it is being eaten. -Ghanian

She who succeeds is reputed wise. -Italian

He who died is praised; he who lives is scolded. -Oromo

He who covers over an offense promotes love, but whoever repeats the matter separates close friends. -Biblical

She who trusts in God will not spend the night hungry. -Oromo

She who treads the path of love walks a thousand meters as if it were only one. -Japanese

He who cries today that he has no bread will cry again tomorrow because he isn't hungry. -German

He who does not commit follies in his youth commits them in his old age. -Swedish

He who continually uses an axe, must keep it sharp. -Hausa

She who takes one sip isn't satisfied. -Hausa

One who cannot pick up an ant and wants to pick up an elephant
will some day see his folly. -Jabo

The appearance of the wise differs from that of the fool. -Yoruba

What cleverness hides, cleverness will reveal. -Fulani

By the time the fool has learned to play the game,
the players have dispersed. -Ashanti

However foolish the monkey it will not play with the thorn tree. -Hausa

The heart of a fool is in his mouth
and the mouth of the wise man is in his heart. -Ethiopian

You become wise when you begin to run out of money. -Ghanian

The fool speaks, the wise man listens. -Ethiopian

From the well of envy, only a fool drinks the water. -Nigerois

The fool who owns an ox is seldom recognized as a fool. -South African

A fool is a wise man's ladder. -South African

A person does not become clever by carrying books along. -Swahili

Wisdom cannot be bought for money. -Ovambo

The man whose sheep gets loose twice is a fool. -Ghanian

A fool and water follow where they are led. -Oromo

Beauty and money make fools of people. -Oromo

All wisdom is from God. -Ghanian

A wise person speaks only once. -Oromo

Families who have wise persons will overcome difficulties and sorrows. -Oromo

People think that the poor are not as wise as the rich,
for if a man be wise, why is he poor? -African

189

The anger of the prudent never shows. -Burmese

Boasting begins where wisdom stops. -Japanese

Even a fool may sometimes have one accomplishment. -Korean

Fools and scissors may be put to use. -Japanese

The fool continues procrastinating, the wise man waits a fit occasion. -Turkish

Though fools are told a thousand times, the thing is useless. -Tamil

The wise hawk conceals his talons. -Japanese

The wise man does at first what the fool does at last. -Hindi

An imbecile can manage his own affairs better than a wise man the affairs of other people. -Arabian

The fool's excuse is bigger than the mistake he made. -Iranian

Wisdom consists of ten parts—nine parts of silence and one part with few words. -Arabian

The fool does what he can't avoid, the wise man avoids what he can't do. -Chinese

A clever person turns great troubles into little ones and little ones into none at all. -Chinese

Though the snake be small, it is still wise to hit it with a big stick. -Indian

A wise man adapts himself to circumstances, as water shapes itself to the vessel that contains it. -Chinese

Wise men are never in a hurry. -Chinese

You need your wits about you the most when you are dealing with an idiot. -Chinese

Silence is a fence around wisdom. -Hebrew

When the wise man gets angry, he stops being wise. -Hebrew

Wealth gets in the way of wisdom. -Japanese

There is no need to fasten a bell to a fool,
he is sure to tell his own tale. -Danish

Someone else's calamity doesn't add to your own wisdom. -Russian

The feast passes and the fool remains. -Italian

If folly were a pain, there would be groaning in every house. -Spanish

A fool may throw a stone into a well
which a hundred wise men cannot pull out. -English

Fools tie knots and wise men loosen them. -English

If a fool has a hump nobody notices it; if the wise man has a pimple
everybody talks about it. -Russian

You cannot be very smart if you have never done anything foolish. -French

One fool always finds a greater fool to admire him. -French

One fool in a play is more than enough. -English

The fool wanders, the wise man travels. -English

God sells wisdom for labor and suffering. -Russian

A wise man will make more opportunities than he finds. -English

The wise man cannot recover the stone
which the fool threw into the well. -Serbo-Croatian

You may be a wise man though you can't make a watch. -English

A nod for a wise man, and a rod for a fool. -English

Where one is wise, two are happy. -English

Wisdom Is easy to carry but difficult to gather. -Czech

Fools are like other folks as long as they are silent. -Danish

If you go only once round the room,
you are wiser than he who sits still. -Estonian

He who claps his hands for the fool to
dance is no better than the fool. -Yoruba

She who wants to be a dragon must
eat many little snakes. -Chinese

She who wants a mule without fault
must walk on foot. -Spanish

He who chastises not his children is
himself at last chastised. -Turkish

She who walks in silence quarrels
with nobody. -Swahili

She who turns to look a second
time will lose nothing. -Chinese

He who carries a basket of lime leaves
footprints wherever he stops. -Chinese

He who cannot speak well of his trade
does not understand it. -French

She who waits for chance
may wait a year. -Yoruba

He who carries nothing
loses nothing. -French

The heart of the wise man lies quiet like limpid water. -Cameroonian

A little nod is enough for the wise man; an ass needs a fist. -Moroccan

Wisdom does not come overnight. -Somalian

The wise person uses a pesewa to get thirty-six dollars
from a foolish person. -Ghanian

For a case one goes to a wise person; for a battle one goes to a hero. -Oromo

If you are stupid, you will be killed. -Ghanian

If the fool knows nothing at all,
at least he knows all about eating fufu. -Ghanian

Don't advise a fool and tell nothing to a madman. -Oromo

Although the horse is stupid,
it does not follow that the rider is stupid. -Ghanian

One sends a wise person, not a long-legged person. -Ghanian

If a foolish person chews on a stick, he chews on it with his back teeth. -Ghanian

If you do good to someone and he does not do good to you,
then he considers you a fool. -Ghanian

"All the handsome men are related to me so I ended up with a fool." -Oromo

A wise person cannot save a decaying country;
manure cannot save an eroding land. -Oromo

People who are foolish have nine dogs for barking when one is enough. -Oromo

They make the fool laugh and then count his teeth. -Oromo

Though he heard it in the market place, the fool hides it from his wife. -Oromo

What they advise the fool, the wise person grasps. -Oromo

Whatever a fool and a sheet of paper get hold of, they never give up. -Oromo

When a wise person goes bad he cannot be corrected. -Oromo

Silence is music to a wise man. -Turkish

The wise man says what he knows;
the fool doesn't know what he is saying. -Turkish

Wise people keep their mouth closed, strong people
keep their arms folded. -Vietnamese

A great sage is often taken for a great fool. -Japanese

Instruct a wise man and he will be wiser still. -Biblical

A wise son brings joy to his father,
but a foolish son grief to his mother. -Biblical

Even a fool is thought wise if he keeps silent. -Biblical

When scholars vie,
wisdom mounts. -Hebrew

Better a wise man's servant than an idiot's master. -Vietnamese

Wine is a mocker and beer a brawler;
whoever is led astray by them is not wise. -Biblical

A wise man has great power,
and a man of knowledge increases strength. -Biblical

As a dog returns to its vomit, so a fool repeats his folly. -Biblical

A fool gives full vent to his anger, but a wise man
keeps himself under control. -Biblical

The wise man has eyes in his head,
while the fool walks in the darkness. -Biblical

Like the crackling of thorns under the pot,
so is the laughter of fools. -Biblical

The words of the wise are like goads, their collected sayings
like firmly embedded nails --given by one Shepherd. -Biblical

To the world wisdom is folly; to the wise the world is foolish. -Indian

Every prudent man acts out of knowledge,
but a fool exposes his folly. -Biblical

194 As the ignorant keep on talking, the wise man arrives at a conclusion. -Iranian

An idiot is eloquent when he stays silent. -Japanese

Sometimes the whole nation has to pay for
the foolish deed of one man. -German

A fool by chance may say a wise thing. -Dutch

Be wise, but pretend to be ignorant. -Russian

It is better to weep with wise men than to laugh with fools. -Spanish

Fool's paradises are wise men's purgatories. -English

The most stupid peasants get the largest potatoes. -Swedish

If you will not hear reason, it will surely rap your knuckles. -English

There is no wise response to a foolish remark. -Slovakian

The wise man will be cheated only once. -Laplandish

Most things have two handles
and a wise man takes hold of the best. -English

When wisdom fails, luck helps. -Danish

A fool looks to the beginning, a wise man regards the end. -English

A wise man and a fool together know more than a wise man alone. -Italian

When a wise man talks to a fool, two fools are talking. -Yiddish

Stupid solutions that succeed are still stupid solutions. -Yiddish

A wise man hears one word and understands two. -Yiddish

Reason governs the wise man, and cudgels the fool. -English

Though the speaker be a fool, let the hearer be wise. -Spanish

He would be wise who knew all things beforehand. -Dutch

For every wagon load of wisdom there are two of stupidity. -Serbo-Croatian

When the ass is too happy he
begins dancing on the ice. -Dutch

When the cat and mouse agree,
the grocer is ruined. -Iranian

When the crane attempts to
dance with the horse it gets
broken bones. -Danish

What lowers itself is ready to
fall. -African

What is true of the buffalo's
bowels is true of the cow's
bowels. -Vietnamese

Whatever accomplishment you
boast of in the world, there is
someone better than you. -Hausa

What you lose on the cost
you will gain in the wear.
-Malaysian

When goodness is planning to do
something, then crookedness follows
him seeking to join. -Ghanian

When a whore repents she becomes a matchmaker. -Egyptian

What one desires is always
better than what one has.
-Ethiopian

Every dog rests at his own door. -Hausa

When we compete in working, our hands quicken. -Yoruba

The mind of a workman is in his stomach. -Moroccan

Sleep is the cousin of death. -Congolese

Work and you will be strong; sit and you will smell. -Moroccan

If you don't want to resign yourself to poverty, resign yourself to work. -Hausa

First work, then wages. -Swahili

A man with **too much ambition** cannot sleep in peace. -Ghanian

The work of the poor and the work of the wind are useless. -Oromo

Sleep is an enemy. -Basotho

People working on the slope of a mountain
do not look at the buttocks of one another. -Ghanian

Work that can be finished in one day is not real work. -Ghanian

Having no one to play with is worse than poverty. -Ghanian

If the bag tears, then the shoulders get a rest. -Ghanian

If the mouth doesn't get work to do, it gets into trouble. -Ghanian

After hard work one sets up the griddle. -Oromo

The morning is for work; the rest of the day depends on the person. -Oromo

Work awaits a worker. -Oromo

Resting does not complete a journey between two villages. -Nkundu-Mongo

The goat relaxing its tongue grazes on thorny leaves. -Oromo

197

A stupid act entails doing the work twice over. -Burmese

To be for one day entirely at leisure
is to be for one day an immortal. -Chinese

A dog has nothing to do, and no time to rest. -Tamil

Labor is the key to rest. -Hindustani

Sleep is a priceless treasure; the more one has of it, the better it is. -Chinese

Poor men sleep the best. -Japanese

You won't get sick if you have plenty of work. -Japanese

Work is the source of all good. -Thai

The heart at rest sees a feast in everything. -Indian

Pleasure seekers have no leisure. -Japanese

It Is only in your coffin that you sleep really well. -Indian

All hard work brings a profit, but mere talk leads only to poverty. -Biblical

Do you see a man skilled in his work? He will serve before kings. -Biblical

Work is afraid of a resolute man. -Chinese

Do not wear yourself out to get rich;
have the wisdom to show restraint. -Biblical

The sleep of a laborer is sweet, whether he eats little or much, but the
abundance of a rich man permits him no sleep. -Biblical

Lack of work brings a thousand diseases. -Hindi

The hard work of a hundred years may be destroyed in an hour. -Chinese

What does man gain from all his labor at which he toils under the sun? -Biblical

The worker deserves his wages. -Biblical

Where the body wants to rest, there the legs must carry it. -Polish

A change of work is as good as a rest. -Irish

Idle folks have the least leisure. -English

Labor has a bitter root, but a sweet taste. -Danish

A life of leisure and a life of laziness are two things. -English

Many a man labors for the day he will never live to see. -Danish

The work will teach you how to do it. -Estonian

The misery is that you have to ruin your day with work. -German

If the devil catch a man idle, he'll set him at work. -English

With hard work, you can get fire out of a stone. -Dutch

One never tires working for oneself. -Russian

Work is half of health. -Swedish

A good rest is half the job. -Yugoslavian

Poverty passes by an industrious man's door. -Greek

Rest comes from unrest, and unrest from rest. -German

Rest is good after the work is done. -Danish

A trade makes you a king but robs you of leisure. -Yiddish

Because of a stupid head the legs have no rest. -Russian

A short rest is always good. -Danish

Rest in reason is not time lost. -Norwegian

He who has luck will have the
winds blow him his firewood. -Libyan

She who wears a smile instead of
worrying is always the strongest.
-Japanese

He who builds in a bog
must not be sparing with
the stakes. -Russian

He who brags about his sins will
be rejected by the grave. -Oromo

He who brings trouble on his
family will inherit only wind.
-Biblical

She who wants to be famous
will have many a sleepless night. -Tunisian

She who wants to talk with
the dogs must learn to bark.
-Romanian

She who was busy with two
things drowned. -Bemba

She who wants to build
high must dig deep.
-Mongolian

He who builds according
to every man's advice will
have a crooked house.
-Danish

If the fight is tomorrow, why then clench your fist today? -Cameroonian

When you wait for tomorrow it never comes.
When you don't wait for it tomorrow still comes. -Guinean

Tomorrow is very close. -Fulani

Nobody knows the future. -Ghanian

You take away the thing from the one who will go tomorrow
and give it to the one who will go today. -Ghanian

The way a finger enters today, a hand enters tomorrow. -Oromo

If you want a loan, come tomorrow. -Lugbara

A man knows not whether he will see tomorrow. -Efik

Do not put off today's work till tomorrow. -Ovambo

"Tomorrow, tomorrow" and before tomorrow comes the child is old. -Oromo

The mistake committed in the past is a joke today. -Oromo

Things of yesterday, they do not inquire about today. -Oromo

Yesterday's drunkenness will not quench today's thirst. -Egyptian

Yesterday and the day before yesterday are not like today. -Swahili

It is to the ungrateful we say, "Remember the past!" -Ghanian

The olden times are what we see today. -Ghanian

The blind person speaks about the things of the past, when he had eyes. -Oromo

When asked, "Didn't you decide yesterday?"
They answered, "Didn't we pass a night sleeping?" -Oromo

An old man was in the world before a chief was born. -Ghanian

If they say something is coming, they mean what has come before. -Ghanian

The rich man plans for the future,
but the poor man for the present. -Chinese

It may be a fire today—tomorrow it will be ashes. -Arabian

They have sowed the seed of the word "tomorrow"
and it has not germinated. -Arabian

Men see only the present; heaven sees the future. -Chinese

Who has ever seen tomorrow? -Iranian

Say what you have to say, tomorrow. -Japanese

Do not boast about tomorrow,
for you do not know what a day may bring forth. -Biblical

Learn the future by looking at things past. -Tamil

The fortuneteller does not know his own future. -Japanese

Today's wine I drink today; tomorrow's sorrow I bear tomorrow. -Chinese

Never admit that there is a tomorrow. -Japanese

It is in vain to look for yesterday's fish in the house of the otter. -Hindi

A book is a good friend when it lays bare the errors of the past. -Indian

Consider the past and you will know the future. -Chinese

The past is as clear as a mirror, the future as dark as lacquer. -Chinese

All the past died yesterday; the future is born today. -Chinese

Yesterday, today and tomorrow—these are the three days of man. -Chinese

What was a deep pool yesterday is but a shallows today. -Japanese

Yesterday's lovely flower is but a dream today. -Japanese

A sponge to wipe away the past; a rose to sweeten the present;
a kiss to greet the future. -Arabian

Tomorrow is untouched. -English

Pain past is pleasure. -English

Anger is the only thing to put off till tomorrow. -Slovakian

When God says "today," the devil says "tomorrow." -German

He that saves something today will have something tomorrow. -Dutch

Nobody is too young to die tomorrow. -Swedish

One today is worth two tomorrows. -English

He that falls today may be up again tomorrow. -English

Give me today
and you may
keep tomorrow. -Greek

Tomorrow's remedy will not ward off the evil of today. -Spanish

If men could foresee the future,
they would still behave as they do now. -Russian

It is too late to call again yesterday. -English

Past labor is pleasant. -English

It is too late to grieve when the chance is past. -English

Every day learns from the one that went before,
but no day teaches the one that follows. -Russian

Things present are judged by things past. -English

He that praises the past blames the present. -Finnish

Past cure, past care. -English

The golden age never was the present age. -English

Time past never returns. -Dutch

When the judge's mule dies, everyone goes to the funeral; when the
judge himself dies, no one does.
-Arabian

Whoever stays awake
longest must blow out the
candle. -Italian

With the help of an "if" you
might put Paris into a bottle.
-French

When you are looking for a country
with no tombstones you will find
yourself in the land of cannibals.
-Madagascan

Who sits on your shoulders
will try to climb on your
head. -Swedish

Whip the saddle and give the
mule something to think about.
-Bulgarian

Who wants a thing is blind to
its faults. -Egyptian

When there is a war be-
tween fire and water, fire
loses. -Spanish

When you can't find peace
within yourself, it's useless to
seek it elsewhere. -French

Whenever women say
good-bye they always hang
around for a while. -German

A cow among calves does not grow old. -Ovambo

Old frogs like croaking. -Ovambo

Instruction in youth is like engraving in stones. -Moroccan

When you get older you keep warm
with the wood you gathered as a youth. -Bambara

If a young woman says no to marriage
just wait until her breasts sag. -Burundi

Man is like palm-wine: when young, sweet but without strength;
in old age, strong but harsh. -Congolese

Old age does not announce itself. -Zulu

You do not teach the paths of the forest to an old gorilla. -Congolese

It is easy to become a monk in one's old age. -Ethiopian

Old age devours your youth. -Kenyan

The young cannot teach tradition to the old. -Yoruba

Those who are handsome when growing up
are often ugly when growing old. -Oromo

A young person and a monkey suit one another. -Ghanian

A journey should be made in the morning;
a marriage when people are young. -Oromo

The thing that was crooked while young will not
be straightened by age. -Oromo

Youth is beauty, even in cattle. -Egyptian

Hunger makes a youngster old, repletion makes an old man young. -Hausa

Old palm nuts are not used to make soup. -Ghanian

The old person who has lived long can tell things. -Oromo

A kind person does not grow old. -Basotho

Childhood is a crown of roses, old age a crown of thorns. -Hebrew

The older ginger and cinnamon become,
the more pungent is their flavor. -Chinese

Even if we study to old age we shall not finish learning. -Chinese

Youth is a kind of illness cured only by the passing years. -Arabian

The household with its own elder has indeed its own adornment. -Chinese

There are old men of three years old and children of a hundred. -Japanese

If you wish to succeed, consult three old people. -Chinese

Train a child in the way he should go,
and when he is old he will not turn from it. -Biblical

An Old lion will be mocked by the dogs. -Arabian

Better a poor but wise youth than an old but foolish king who no longer
knows how to take warning. -Biblical

Remember your Creator in the days of your youth,
before the days of trouble come. -Biblical

Youth comes never again. -Korean

In the freshness of youth a woman is like a gilded statue, but when youth
has faded she looks like a beehive on a rainy day. -Vietnamese

Many old camels carry the hides of young ones. -Hebrew

Old men for consultation, young men for quarrels. -Japanese

A young snake is more poisonous and vigorous than an old one. -Tamil

A woman is young till she bears a child,
and cloth is new till it is washed. -Tamil

Young, one wears flowers; old, one bears disease. -Vietnamese

Youth and wine are like a whip to a galloping horse. -Japanese

Youth easily grows old yet becomes learned with difficulty. -Japanese

If you want to avoid old age, hang yourself in youth. -Yiddish

Old birds are not caught with new nets. -Italian

If the young man would, and the old man could,
there would be nothing undone. -English

Young men think old men fools,
but old men know the young men are. -English

High climbers and deep swimmers never grow old. -German

There is no nail varnish that can make old hands look younger. -German

Old age is a disease that you die from. -German

If you want to be a hundred you must start young. -Russian

Old age is no protection against foolishness. -German

The oldest trees bear the softest fruits. -German

The heart that loves is always young. -Greek

An old coachman loves the crack of the whip. -Dutch

The young may die, the old must. -Dutch

Praise the young and they will blossom. -Irish

Old truths, old laws, old friends, old books, and old wine are best. -Polish

The young should be taught, the old should be honored. -Swedish

Time is the rider that breaks youth. -English

If youth knew what age would crave, it would both get and save. -English

A young tree bends; an old tree breaks. -Yiddish

A young trooper should have an old horse. -English

She who would visit a vice, never
has far to travel. -Arabian

She who would have a bone
from a dog must give the
meat instead. -Norwegian

She who won't be advised, can't be helped. -German

She who would gather roses
must not fear thorns. -Dutch

He who admits to his ignorance shows
it once only; he who tries to hide it
shows it frequently. -Japanese

He who begins badly, ends badly. -Spanish

He who begins many things finishes few. -Italian

He who begins and does not
finish loses his labor. -French

He who begins early helps himself a lot. -Bemba

She who works on the highway
will have many advisers. -Spanish

Women should stop using lime in
their bath water because even the red
ant stinks. -Ghanian

You can't climb a mountain
by a level road. -Norwegian

You can't blame the axe for
the noise made by the chicken
you are about to slaughter.
-Madagascan

You need not look after
the hoofs of dead horses.
-Romanian

You can't put two saddles
on the same horse.
-Mongolian

You don't really see the world
if you only look through your
own window. -Ukrainian

Your secret is your blood—
when you shed it you die.
-Berber

You don't milk a cow with
your hands in your pockets.
-Russian

You cannot breathe through
another man's nose.
-Vietnamese

You must have good luck
to catch hares with a drum.
-Danish

Bibliography

Daniel Crump Buchanan, Japanese Proverbs and Sayings
(Norman, Oklahoma, University of Oklahoma Press, 1965).

J.G. Christaller, Three Thousand Six Hundred Ghanian Proverbs (Edwin Mellen
Press, 1990). On "The Wisdom Of African Proverbs," Stan Nussbaum Ed.,
Version 1.2, 1998, Global Mapping International.

George Cotter, Ethiopian Wisdom: Proverbs and Sayings of the Oromo People
(1996). On "The Wisdom Of African Proverbs," Stan Nussbaum Ed.,
Version 1.2, 1998, Global Mapping International.

Harold V. Cordry, The Multicultural Dictionary of Proverbs
(Jefferson, North Carolina, McFarland & Company, 1997).

Albert Dalfovo, Lugbara Wisdom (1996) On "The Wisdom Of African Proverbs,"
Stan Nussbaum Ed., Version 1.2, 1998, Global Mapping International.

Henry Davidoff, A World Treasury of Proverbs from Twenty-five Languages
(New York, Random House, 1946).

Gerd de Ley, International Dictionary of Proverbs
(New York, Hippocrene Books, 1998).

Wilma S. Jaggard Hobgood, Proverbs of the Nkundo-Mongo Tribes in Belgian
Congo, 1949. On "The Wisdom Of African Proverbs," Stan Nussbaum Ed.,
Version 1.2, 1998, Global Mapping International.

Patrick Ibekwe, Wit & Wisdom of Africa
(Trenton, New Jersey, New Internationalist Publications, Ltd., 1998).

Wolfgang Mieder, The Prentice-Hall Encyclopedia of World Proverbs
(New York, MJF Books, 1986).

Makali I. Mokitimi, The Voice of the People: Proverbs of the Basotho (1996). On
"The Wisdom Of African Proverbs," Stan Nussbaum Ed.,
Version 1.2, 1998, Global Mapping International.

Kim Yong-chol, Proverbs, East and West
(Elizabeth, New Jersey, Hollym International Corp., 1991).

John S. Rohsenow, ABC Dictionary of Chinese Proverbs
(Honolulu, University of Hawai'i Press, 2002).

Mineke Schipper, Never Marry A Woman With Big Feet: Women In Proverbs From
Around The World (New Haven, Connecticut, Yale University Press, 2003).

Arthur H. Smith, Proverbs And Common Sayings From The Chinese
(New York, Dover Publications Inc., 1965).

Perhaps proverbs from this collection, or observations from your own experience have inspired you. Don't keep your thoughts to yourself! Visit Triku.com, compose your own copyrighted trikus and share them with the world.